CASTLE AT DOLPHIN BAY

**Amidst a struggle for inheritance and title,
love and family triumph—against all odds!**

Twin sisters
Kirsty McMahon is travelling to
Australia with her heavily pregnant widowed
twin Susie, to help her locate the
baby's great-uncle.

A castle in…Australia!
Angus Douglas is no ordinary uncle—
he's a Scottish earl with a *faux*-medieval
castle and millions in the bank. The adventure
has only just begun…

A whole lot of romance…
Kirsty and Susie are suddenly embroiled in an
inheritance battle and a bid to save the castle
from destruction, yet amidst all this the twins
each find the one big thing that has been
missing from their lives.

**CASTLE AT DOLPHIN BAY
Read the second and final story in this
compelling, heartwarming and intriguing
tale of love, riches and aristocracy
from this award-winning author in
THE HEIR'S CHOSEN BRIDE, coming
next month in Mills & Boon®
Tender Romance™.**

Dear Reader,

I love ancient castles, handsome lords in kilts of ancient tartan, and bagpipes on the battlements. My Scottish friends, however, tell me a feisty heroine is more likely to be hidden by fog or eaten by midges than she is to find the man of her dreams on yon Scottish parapet.

My Australian climate does have some advantages.

Fine, I thought. I'm a fiction writer. I'll transfer my Scottish castle to my favourite place in the world—Australia's New South Wales coast. With a wave of my magic wand I've therefore brought the romance of Scotland to the turquoise waters of today's Dolphin Bay. Add a family feud, a fortune to be won, a double set of twins and a couple of very sexy heroes… It's far too much for one book so I've spread the fun over two.

My Castle at Dolphin Bay duo, starting with *The Doctor's Proposal,* has every element that good romance requires—including Queen Victoria in the bathroom and a murderer out on the bay. So far it's two books—the next being *The Heir's Chosen Bride*—but if you enjoy them please let me know—via www.marionlennox.com. I may be forced to write another. And another. :-)

Happy reading

Marion Lennox

THE DOCTOR'S PROPOSAL

BY
MARION LENNOX

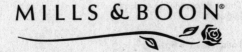

MILLS & BOON®

First published in Great Britain 2006
Harlequin Mills & Boon Limited,
Eton House, 18-24 Paradise Road, Richmond, Surrey TW9 1SR

© Marion Lennox 2006

Standard ISBN 0 263 84736 5
Promotional ISBN 0 263 85097 8

Set in Times Roman 10¼ on 11½ pt.
03-0606-54828

Printed and bound in Spain
by Litografia Rosés, S.A., Barcelona

CHAPTER ONE

How did you knock on the front door of a medieval castle? And what was such a castle doing in a remote Australian fishing community?

Dr Kirsty McMahon was worried and tired and it was starting to rain. The castle doors looked as if they'd take a battering ram to open them, and using the incongruous intercom-thing produced nothing. Her tentative knock sounded ridiculous. She knocked harder and gave a hopeful shout but there was no response.

Enough. She'd been stupid to come. Susie was complaining of cramp. She and her twin would find a hotel in Dolphin Bay and broach the castle walls in the morning. If she could get Susie back here.

Then she paused as a sudden flurry of barking sounded on the other side of the gates. Was someone coming?

The vast timber doors opened an inch, and then wider. A lanky brown dog of indiscriminate parentage nosed its way out. A hand gripped its collar. A man's hand.

She took a step back. This place seemed straight out of a Gothic novel. The castle was set high on the cliffs above the sea, with purple-hazed mountains ringing the rear. In the mist of early evening, Kirsty was almost expecting to be met by a pack of ancient hunting dogs, anchored to armoured warriors with battle-axes.

'Boris, if you jump up on anyone you'll be toast.'

She blinked. The owner of the voice didn't sound like an axe-toting warrior. The voice sounded…nice?

The doors swung wider and she decided the adjective *nice* wasn't strong enough.

Her warrior was gorgeous.

Six feet two. Mid-thirties maybe? Aran sweater, faded jeans and battered boots. Deep brown, crinkly hair, ruffled just the way she liked it in her men.

Her men? Robert? The thought almost made her smile and she had no difficulty at all turning her attention back to her warrior.

What else? He had a craggy face, strongly boned and weathered. His eyes smiled at the edges even when he wasn't smiling. His body was…excellent.

Oh, for heaven's sake, she was standing outside a ridiculous Australian castle thinking lustful thoughts about a strange man's body? All her life she'd fought to stay in control, and now, when everything was teetering, the last thing she needed was the complication of a male. Back home she was dating nice, safe Robert, who'd stay being nice and safe for as long as she wanted. She was in control. She was married to medicine.

But her warrior was definitely gorgeous.

'Um…hello,' she tried.

The stranger was hauling his dog back, giving her a chance to catch her breath. Behind the man and dog she could see the castle forecourt. This, then, was why there'd been no response. She'd knocked on what was essentially the fortress gates.

And behind the gates… The castle was a lacy confection of gleaming white stone, turrets and battlements. Kirsty was practically gaping. It was so ridiculously seventeenth-century-meets-now that it was fantastic. It was also set so far back from the gates that, if the intercom wasn't working, it must have been sheer luck that anyone had heard her call.

She needed to stop gaping.

'What can I do for you?' the man asked, and she attempted to sound coherent. Sort of.

'My sister and I have come to see Ang—the earl.'

'I'm sorry, but His Lordship isn't receiving visitors.' It was a brisk denial, made in a hurry as he pushed the gates closed again.

She stuck her foot forward.

Mistake. These gates weren't built so that a five-feet-four doctor of not very impressive stature could block them with one toe.

She yelped. Her warrior swore, and the gate swung wide again.

'Did I hurt you?'

'Yes.'

'You shouldn't have put your foot there.'

'You were closing the gate in my face.'

He sighed. They both inspected her foot for a moment, waiting for it to do something interesting, but she was wearing solid trainers. And she'd hauled her foot out fast. Maybe she'd suffered nothing worse than a minor bruise.

'I'm sorry,' the man said, and as his voice softened she thought again just how gorgeous he was. His voice was deep and resonant, with the lazy drawl of an Australian accent. Well, what had she expected in Australia? But he did seem to be…caring.

And his caring tone tugged something inside her that hadn't been tugged for a long, long time.

She must be more tired than she'd thought, she decided, surprising herself with the depth of her reaction. Caring? She was the one who was doing the caring.

'His Lordship isn't up to seeing visitors,' he was saying, still in the gentle, reasonable tone that did weird things to her insides. 'And he doesn't see tourists at any time.'

'We're not tourists.'

'We?'

She motioned to the car where Susie was peering out anxiously from the passenger seat. 'My sister and I.'

'You're American.'

'Good call,' she told him. 'But we're still not tourists.'

'But you still can't see His Lordship.' Once more the gates started to close.

'We're family,' she said quickly, and the gates stilled.

The man's face stilled.

'What did you say?'

'We're a part of Angus's family,' she told him. 'We've come all the way from America to see him.'

There was a deathly silence. She had been wrong, she thought when she'd decided this man's eyes smiled all the time. They weren't smiling now. He suddenly looked cold, disdainful and very, very angry.

'You're too early,' he told her, and he hauled his dog back behind him as if she was something that might be infectious. 'I thought the vultures would be arriving soon, and here you are. But Angus is still alive.'

He didn't even look to see where her foot was.

The gate slammed shut against her.

Ten minutes and a Thermos of tea later they were still none the wiser. Kirsty had returned to the car and filled Susie in on the details.

'Well, at least we're at the right place,' Kirsty told her sister. 'But I don't know who the sentry is. A son?'

'I was sure Angus didn't have sons.' Susie wriggled deeper into the passenger seat, trying to get comfortable, no mean feat at eight months pregnant. Kirsty's twin had been sitting still for too long, but she hadn't wanted to get out when they'd arrived. It had been too much trouble. Everything was too much trouble for Susie, Kirsty thought grimly, and, instead of making it better, these last few weeks had made it worse. Clinical depression was crippling.

More. It was terrifying.

'So what do we do?' Susie asked, but she asked as if it didn't matter too much what Kirsty replied.

Over to Kirsty. As always.

Obediently Kirsty thought about it. What could they do? Retreat to town and try and gain access again in the morning? Telephone? They should have telephoned in the first place, but she hadn't been sure they'd reach here.

She glanced across at Susie. Exhaustion was washing over her twin's face and she knew she had no choice.

This had turned into a disastrous expedition, she thought bleakly, but back home in New York it had seemed reasonable. Even sensible. For Susie, the last few months had been appalling, and Kirsty had fought every way she'd known to haul her twin out of a clinical depression that was becoming almost suicidal.

Two years ago Susie had married Rory Douglas. Rory was a Scottish Australian who'd decided two minutes after meeting Susie that America—and Susie—was home. It had been a bliss-fully happy marriage. Six months ago Kirsty's twin had been glowing with early pregnancy, and she and her Rory had been joyfully preparing to live happily ever after.

But then had come the car crash. Rory had been killed in-stantly. Susie had been dreadfully physically injured, but her mental state was worse.

Psychiatrists hadn't helped. Nothing had helped.

'Why not visit Australia?' Kirsty had suggested at last, flailing for answers. 'You know so little about Rory's back-ground. I know his parents are dead and he didn't get on with his brother, but at least we can visit where he was born. Dolphin Bay? Are there really dolphins? All we know is that it's on the coast somewhere south of Sydney. It sounds exciting. I can take leave from the hospital. Let's go on a fact-finding tour so you'll be able to tell your baby where his daddy came from.'

It had seemed a sensible idea. Sure, Susie was pregnant and the injuries to her back meant she was still using a wheelchair most of the time, but Kirsty was a doctor. She could care for her. Because Susie had been married to an Australian, she was covered for health costs in Australia. At seven months pregnant she had only just been able to make the journey before airline restrictions stopped travel, but Kirsty had decided even if they got stuck it would be no disaster. If the baby was to be born in Australia, Susie would have her own little Australian. It'd be great.

But Susie had been apathetic from the start, and nothing had gone right. Their plane had no sooner touched down in Sydney than Susie had shown signs of early labour. What had followed had been four weeks in Sydney on a medical knife edge, with Susie's depression deepening with the enforced idleness.

But at least the baby had stayed *in situ*. Now Susie was eight months pregnant, and if she did go into labour it wasn't a major drama. Enough with doing nothing, Kirsty had decreed in desperation. They'd finally headed for their destination, travelling in careful, easy stages so they could see the sights as they went.

But all Kirsty had achieved had been more apathy from Susie. And now they stared at the imposing fortress and Susie's expression of bewilderment echoed what was in Kirsty's own heart.

'Why didn't Rory tell me his uncle was an earl?' Susie whispered. 'And to live in a place like this… I never would have come if I'd known this.'

It had been a shock, Kirsty acknowledged. They'd arrived in Dolphin Bay that afternoon, tried the local post office for information and had been stunned by their reception.

'Angus Douglas? That'll be His Lordship you're wanting. The earl.'

'Angus Douglas is an earl?' Kirsty had demanded, and the postmistress had smiled, propped her broad elbows on the counter and prepared to chat.

'Ooh, yes. Dolphin Bay's answer to royalty is our Angus. He's the Earl of Loganaich, he tells us, but the Loganaich part of him is long gone.'

'Loganaich,' Kirsty had said, not understanding, and the lady had needed no more encouragement to expand.

'Apparently his family's castle burned to the ground back

in Scotland,' she told them. 'Lord Angus says it was a nasty, draughty place and no great loss. He's not all that sentimental, His Lordship. Except when it comes to wearing kilts. Ooh, you should see him in a kilt. Anyway, Lord Angus and his brothers left Scotland when they were not much more than teenagers, and two of them—the two eldest—came here.'

'Tell us about them,' Kirsty said faintly, and the lady proceeded to do just that.

'Lord Angus married a nurse during the war,' she said, pointing to a community notice-board. A yellowing newspaper clipping showed an elderly lady at what seemed to be some sort of village fête. 'That's Deirdre, God rest her soul. A lovely, lovely lady.' She sniffed and it was obvious to Kirsty why the fading newspaper was still on the board. This was personal loss.

'Did they have children?' she asked, and was met by a shake of the head that was almost fierce.

'They had no kiddies but they were happy.' The postmistress groped for a handkerchief and blew her nose. 'Deirdre only died two years ago and it broke His Lordship's heart. It broke all our hearts. And now His Lordship's alone in his old age. Doc tells me he's not good. Doc's doing all he can do but there's only so much one doctor can do.'

'Did you say…His Lordship…had brothers?' Kirsty asked cautiously, abandoning the tangent of an overworked doctor for the moment, and got a grimace for reply.

'The brother we knew was a bit…erratic,' the postmistress told them. 'And he married a girl who was worse. They had two boys, Rory and Kenneth. The boys were born here but the family left soon after. The boys came here on school holidays, just for a bit of stability. Deirdre and Angus loved them to bits, but from what I hear Kenneth was too like his dad ever to be peaceable. Kenneth fought with Rory all the time. Finally Rory went to America to get away from him. Then a few months ago we heard he died in a car crash. His Lordship was devastated. Kenneth still visits, but he's not liked locally. We won't be calling him Lord Kenneth when Angus dies, that's for sure.' Her mouth tightened in a grim line. 'Titles are all very well when you're loved, like Lord Angus is, but Kenneth… Ugh.'

'But…Angus is still an earl,' Susie whispered, dazed by this surfeit of information, and the postmistress looked sympathetically at Susie in her wheelchair, and grimaced.

'Seems ridiculous, doesn't it? He doesn't like being called it. He says just Angus is good enough for him. But we like to call him Lord Angus among ourselves—or Lord Douglas when we're being formal. What he and Deirdre did for our town… I can't begin to tell you. Wait till you see his house. Loganaich Castle, we call it, just joking, but the name fits. You need to find it? I'll draw you a map.'

Rory's Uncle Angus an earl? Loganaich Castle?

Susie had come close to going home then—and now, sitting in the car outside the extraordinary mass of gleaming stone that was the new Loganaich Castle, she turned to her twin and her eyes were as bleak as Kirsty had ever seen them.

'Kirsty, what are we doing here? Let's go back to America. We were dumb to come.'

'We've come so far, and you know we can't go back to America now. No airline will take you until after the baby's born. Let's find a bed for the night and come back in the morning.'

'Let's go back to Sydney in the morning.'

'Susie, no. You can't lose every link with Rory.'

'I already have. And you heard the postmistress. Rory had lost any link to his uncle.'

'Rory spoke of Angus and his aunt with affection. The postmistress said Angus was devastated to learn Rory was dead. You have to see him.'

'No.'

'Susie, please…'

'The gates are opening again,' Susie said, in a voice that said she didn't care. 'Someone's coming out. We need to move.'

Kirsty turned to see. There was a dusty Land Rover emerg-

ing from the forecourt out onto the cobbled driveway leading
to the road. Kirsty had driven as close as possible so Susie could
watch her as she'd knocked, and the cobblestones were only a
car-width wide. Their car was blocking the driveway—meaning
the Land Rover had to stop and wait for them to move.

The gates were swinging closed again now behind the Land
Rover. This was apparently a castle with every modern conve-
nience. Electronic sensors must be overriding manual operations.

There was still no access.

OK. They'd go. Kirsty started the engine, and then glanced
one last time at the Land Rover.

The man who'd slammed the gate on her was at the wheel.
His lanky brown dog was sitting beside him. The dog's dumb,
goofy—almost grinning—face was at odds with the man's expression of grim impatience. His fingers were drumming on the
steering-wheel as he waited for her to move.

She hesitated.

The fingers drummed.

The man looked angry as well as impatient.

He wasn't alone in his anger. Kirsty glanced across at her
sister. She wouldn't get Susie back here tomorrow, she thought.
Susie's expression was one of hopelessness.

Where was the laughing, bubbly Susie of a year ago?

Kirsty wanted her back. Fiercely, desperately, Kirsty
mourned her twin.

Her anger doubled. Quadrupled.

Exploded.

She killed the engine.

'What…?' Susie started, but Kirsty was already out of the
car. Her car was half off the cobblestones and there was a
puddle right beside the driver's door. She'd climbed out carefully last time but this time she forgot about the puddle. She
squelched in mud to her ankle.

She hardly noticed. How dared he drum his fingers at her?
In truth her anger was caused by far more than merely

drumming fingers, but the fingers had a matching face, a target for the pent-up grief and frustration and fear of the last few months. Too much emotion had to find a vent somewhere.

The drumming fingers were it.

She marched up to the Land Rover, right to the driver's side. She hauled open the door of the vehicle so hard she almost yanked it off its hinges.

'Right,' she told him. 'Get out. I want some answers and I want them now.'

He should have been home two hours ago.

Dr Jake Cameron had spent the entire day sorting out trouble, and he had more trouble in front of him before he could go home that night. As well as the medicine crowding at him from all sides, there was also the fact that his girls were waiting. The twins were fantastic but he'd stretched their good nature to the limit. Mrs Boyce would have to put them to bed again tonight; she'd be upset at not getting home to Mr Boyce, and he winced at the idea that he'd miss yet another bedtime.

Who needed a bedtime story most? The twins or himself?

The answer was obvious.

'We could all use a good fairy-tale,' he told Boris as he watched the flaming ball of anger stomp along the cobblestones toward him. 'Do godmothers do a line in "Beam me up, Scotty"?'

No godmother arrived, and he couldn't leave. The woman's car was blocking his path and he was forced to stay motionless while she hauled open his door and let him have it with both barrels.

She wanted answers?

'What do you mean, you want answers?' he asked coldly, sliding his long frame out from the vehicle so he could face her anger head on. She'd said she was Angus's family but he'd never seen her before. Who was she?

He would have noticed if he had seen her, he decided. She was five feet three or four, slim, with an open face, clear brown eyes and glossy auburn curls that tangled almost to her collar. Late twenties? he thought. She had to be—and she was lovely. She was dressed in faded, hip-hugging jeans and an oversized waterproof jacket, but her clothes did nothing to dispel his impression that she was lovely.

Apart from her foot. One foot had landed in a puddle. It was the same foot he'd squashed, he remembered, and he looked down and saw the mud and felt repentant.

Then he thought of Angus and he stopped feeling repentant.

'My sister and I have travelled all the way from New York to visit Mr…Lord Douglas,' she snapped. 'We need to see the earl.'

'You mean Angus.' He'd only referred to Angus as His Lordship to intimidate these two into leaving. It hadn't worked so he may as well go back to using Angus. Angus, his friend.

What else could he do for the old man? he wondered as he waited for the virago to speak again. Angus needed oxygen. He needed round-the-clock nursing, and if he didn't get it…

'My sister's not well,' the woman snapped.

So what was new? 'No one's well,' he said bitterly. 'And there's only me to deal with it. I need to do three more house calls before dinner. Can you move your car, please?'

'You're a doctor?' she asked blankly, and he sighed.

'Yes. I'm Dr Jake Cameron, Angus's doctor.'

'You don't look like a doctor.'

'Would you like me to wear a white coat and stethoscope? Here? An hour ago I was shifting cows blocking the track to my next patient. This is not exactly white-coat country.'

'I thought you might have been a nephew.'

'You are indeed a close family,' he said dryly. 'Does your sister need medical attention?'

'No, but—'

'Then, please, move your vehicle. I'm two hours late and you're making me later.'

She wasn't listening. 'Is there anyone else we can talk to?'

'Angus is alone.'

'In that huge house?'

'He's accustomed to it,' he told her. 'But if it'll make you happier, he won't be here much longer. He's being transferred to the Dolphin Bay nursing home tomorrow. It'd be much easier to call there, don't you think? But if you're thinking of pushing him to change his will, don't bother. You bring a lawyer near him and I'll call the police.'

She gazed straight at him, her eyes wide and assessing.

'Why are you being horrible?'

'I'm not being any more horrible than I have to be. Angus is weary to death of family pressure and I'm in a hurry.'

'So be nice to me fast. Tell me why we can't see the earl.'

He sighed. He'd had this family up to his ears. 'Angus has severe breathing difficulties,' he told her. 'He's settled for the night and if you think he's coming downstairs to indulge a couple of money-grubbing—'

'You see, there's the problem,' she said, and her own anger was palpable. 'You're treating us as if we're something lower than pond scum. We don't even know Angus. We never knew he was an earl or that he was living in something that looks like a cross between Disneyland and Camelot. And as for money-grubbing—'

He was hardly listening. He couldn't. He was so late! He'd promised Mavis Hipton that he'd look in on her this afternoon, and he knew she needed more analgesic to make it though the night. Mavis suffered in stoic silence. She wouldn't complain, but he didn't want her suffering because of these two.

He glanced at his watch. Pointedly. 'You said you're family,' he told her. 'Why do you know nothing? You're not making sense.'

'My sister was married to one of Angus's nephews,' she told him, standing square in front of him, making it quite clear he wasn't going anywhere until she had answers. 'Susie's never met her husband's family, and she'd like to.'

'Especially now he's dying,' he snapped. It had only been this afternoon that he'd fielded yet another phone call from

Kenneth, and Kenneth had been palpably pleased to hear that Angus was failing. The phone call had left Jake feeling ill. And now…was this Kenneth's wife?

He didn't have time to care.

'I need to go.'

'We didn't know Angus was dying,' she snapped, her colour mounting. 'As far as we knew, Rory's uncle Angus was as poor as a church mouse, but he's all the family Rory had—except a brother he didn't get on with—so we've come all this way to see him. Of all the appalling things to say, that we're fortune hunters!'

He hesitated at that. For a moment he stopped being angry and forced himself to think. What had she said? *Rory's Uncle Angus.* Not Kenneth, then. Rory. The nephew in the States.

She was so indignant that he was forced to do a bit more fast thinking. OK, maybe he was out of line. Maybe his logic was skewed. Angus was one of his favourite patients, and telling him he had to go into a nursing home had been a really tough call.

Kenneth might be nasty and unbalanced but there was no reason to assume everyone else was.

Maybe these two really were family.

He forced himself to think a bit more. Angus had talked affectionately of his nephew Rory. Jake remembered the old man had been devastated to hear he'd died.

If Rory had been married, then this pair really were part of Angus's family.

Caring family?

The idea that hit him then was so brilliant that it made him blink.

'You really don't know Angus?' he asked, thinking so fast he felt dizzy.

'I told you. No.'

'But you'd like to see him tonight?'

'Yes, but—'

'And maybe stay the night,' he told her, ideas cementing. He hated leaving Angus. He needed a full-time nurse, but Angus refused point blank to have one. With the state of his lungs, leaving him by himself seemed criminal. He should be in hospital but he refused to go. There was a bed at the nursing home available tomorrow and the old man had agreed with reluctance that he'd go then.

Which left tonight.

If he could persuade these two to stay, even if they *were* after the old man's money…

'I'll introduce you,' he told her, doing such a fast backtrack that he startled her.

'What, now?'

'Yes, now. If you promise to stay the night then I'll introduce you.'

She was staring at him like he had a kangaroo loose in the top paddock. 'We can't stay the night.'

'Why not?'

'Well…' She looked at him in astonishment. 'We're not invited.'

'I'm inviting you. Angus needs his family now more than he's ever needed anyone. Tomorrow he's being moved into a nursing home but he needs help now. He has pulmonary fibrosis—he has severely diminished lung capacity and I'm worried he'll collapse and not be able to call for help.' He eyed her without much hope, but it was worth asking anyway. 'I don't suppose either of you is a nurse?'

She eyed him back, with much the same expression as he was using. Like she didn't know what to make of him but she was sure his motives were questionable.

'Why?'

'I told you.' He sighed and glanced at his watch again. 'He's ill. He needs help. If you want to see him…are you prepared to help? If one of you is a nurse…'

'Neither of us is a nurse. Susie is a landscape gardener.'

'Damn,' he said and started turning away.

'But I'm a doctor.'

A doctor.

There was a long pause.

He turned back and looked at her—from the tip of her burnt curls to the toe of her muddy foot.

She was glaring at him.

He wasn't interested in the glare.

A doctor.

'You're kidding me,' he said at last. 'A people doctor?'

'A people doctor.'

A tiny hope was building into something huge, and he tried frantically to quell it.

'You know about lung capacity?'

'We have heard of lungs in America, yes,' she snapped, losing her temper again. 'The last ship into port brought some coloured pictures. The current medical belief in Manhattan is that the lungs appear to be somewhere between the neck and the groin. Unless we've got it wrong? It's different in Australia?'

Whoa. He tried a smile and held his hand up placatingly.

'Sorry. I only meant—'

'Oh, it's fine,' she told him bitterly. 'Who cares what you meant? You've insulted us in every way possible. But...' She hesitated. 'Angus is dying?'

His smile faded. 'He's dying,' he said softly. 'Maybe not tonight, but soon. Much sooner if he's left alone. He's refusing oxygen and pain relief, he has heart trouble as well, he won't let the district nurse near, and if you really are a doctor—'

'If you don't believe me—'

'Sorry.' He needed to do some placating here, he thought. Fast. 'Angus is my friend,' he said softly. 'I'm sorry if I've sounded abrupt but I hate leaving him alone. If you agree to stay here tonight you'll be making up for a lot.'

'Making up for...?'

'Neglect.'

Mistake. 'We have not neglected anyone!' It was practically a yell and he gazed at her in bewilderment. She turned a great colour when she was angry, he thought. Her eyes did this dagger thing that was really cute.

Um…that meant what exactly?

That meant he was being dumb.

Cut it out, he told himself crossly. You have hours of house calls. Move on.

'OK,' he agreed. 'You didn't neglect Angus. You didn't know about Angus. I'll accept that.'

'That's noble of you,' she snapped. She glanced behind to the car, but the woman in the passenger seat didn't appear to be moving. 'Angus really does need help?' she asked. 'Medical help?'

'He really does. Personal as well as medical. Urgently.'

'We'll stay, then,' she told him, and it was his turn to be taken aback.

'Just like that. You don't need to consult your sister?'

'Susie's past making decisions.'

He frowned. 'You said she's ill. What's wrong with her?'

'She's not so ill that she can't stay here the night. I assume there's bedding.'

'There are fourteen bedrooms. Deirdre—Angus's wife—was always social. No one's been in them for years but once a month the housekeeper airs them, just in case.'

She was only listening to what was important. 'So there's room to stay. The bedrooms are on the ground floor?'

'Some of them are, but—'

She wasn't listening to buts. She was moving on. 'Where's the housekeeper?'

'She doesn't live in. She comes in three times a week from Dolphin Bay.'

'He really is alone.'

'I told you.'

'And I heard,' she snapped. 'Fine. Go and tell him we're coming.'

'Who did you say you were?'

'I'm Kirsty McMahon.' She drew herself up to her full five feet four inches and rose on her toes so a bit more was added. 'Dr Kirsten McMahon. My sister, Susan, was married to Rory, His Lordship's nephew.'

'The Rory who was killed.' He hesitated. 'I remember. Kenneth—another of Angus's nephews—told Angus some months ago that his brother had been killed in the States. I'm sorry. But—'

'Just leave it,' she said bitterly. 'All you need to know is that we couldn't care less about any inheritance. So let's just stop with the judgement. Go and tell His Lordship who we are and let me get my sister settled for the night.'

She was gorgeous.

She was a lifesaver.

He left them and, with Boris loping beside him, made his way back into the house. He had keys—something he'd insisted on when Angus had had his last coronary—and he knew the way well, so he left Boris—sternly—at the foot of the stairs and made his way swiftly up to the old man's apartments.

A doctor here. The thought was unbelievable. His mind was racing forward but for now... He had to focus on Angus.

Angus wasn't in bed. He was at the window, staring out at the kitchen garden to the sea beyond. He was a little man, wiry and weathered by years of fishing and gardening; a lifetime's love of the outdoors. Jake remembered him in the full regalia of his Scottish heritage, lord of all he surveyed, and the sight of the shrunken old man in his bathrobe and carpet slippers left an ache that was far from the recommended medical detachment he tried for. He'd miss him so much when he died, but that death would be soon.

He needed a coronary bypass and wouldn't have one. That

was a huge risk factor, but it was his lungs that were killing him. Jake could hear his whistling gasps from the door, signifying the old man's desperate lack of oxygen.

'I thought you were going to bed,' Jake growled, trying to disguise emotion, and Angus looked around and tried to smile.

'There's time and more for bed. It's only five o'clock.'

'Your supper's on the bedside table,' Jake told him, still gruff. He'd brought the meal up himself because if he hadn't, Angus wouldn't eat. He and Angus had been friends for a long time now, and it was so hard to see a friend fade.

'I'll get to it. What brings you back?'

'Could you cope with a couple of visitors?'

'Visitors?'

'Two Americans. Sisters. One of them says she was married to Rory.'

'Rory.' Angus's smile faded. 'My Rory?'

'Your nephew.' Jake hesitated. 'Kenneth's older brother? He must have left for overseas before I came here.' He paused and then as Angus turned back to the window he said gently, 'Tell me about him.'

'I haven't seen Rory for years.'

'You had three nephews,' Jake prodded. He wanted family interest—he wanted any interest—and he was prepared to make himself even later to get it. This had to be his top priority. To see Angus give up on life was heartbreaking, and maybe these two women could be his salvation.

'I'd be having two brothers,' Angus whispered, so softly that Jake had to strain to hear. 'We left Scotland together. Dougal, the youngest, went to America. David and I came here. Dougal and I lost touch a long time ago—yes, there's another nephew somewhere, but I've not met him. But David married here and had Rory and then Kenneth. They moved from Dolphin Bay but the lads came back for holidays.'

'Were they nice kids?' Jake murmured, encouraging him.

'Rory loved this place,' Angus said softly. 'He and I would

be fishing together for hours, and Deidre and I loved him like the son we could never have. But Kenneth…'

Kenneth. Jake couldn't suppress a grimace. It had been a dumb question. Kenneth definitely couldn't have been nice.

'Kenneth was Rory's younger brother.' Angus was struggling hard to breathe. Maybe he shouldn't be talking, but Jake didn't intend to interrupt. There were major issues at stake here—like a ready-made family at the front door. If Kirsty really was a doctor… If he could install her here…

'Kenneth is a troubled young man and I'm sure you can be seeing that,' Angus managed. 'You've met him. He takes after his father. Every time Rory came near there was a fuss, more and more as they got older and Kenneth realised Rory would inherit my title. As if any title matters more than family.'

He paused and fought for a few more breaths. There was an ineffable sadness in his eyes that seemingly had nothing to do with his health. 'Kenneth was so vicious toward Rory that, once his parents died, Rory decided family angst wasn't worth it,' he said sadly. 'He took off to see the world. He's been away these past ten years, and the next thing I knew Kenneth was telling me he was dead. I was so…sorry.'

So maybe Kirsty had been telling the truth, Jake thought. Maybe she did know nothing of Angus. For a moment he regretted he'd made her angry. But then he remembered the flare of crimson in her cheeks and the flash of fire in her brown eyes and he didn't regret it. He found he was almost smiling.

This was looking good, he thought. This was looking excellent. Angus had been fond of Rory. Rory's widow was at the gate, and if Rory's widow was anything like her sister…they could be a breath of fresh air in this place. A breath of life.

'They're outside, waiting,' he said. 'I told them to give me a minute and then follow.'

'Who?' Angus was lost in his thoughts, and was suddenly confused.

'Rory's widow and her sister.'

'Rory's widow,' he repeated.

'So it seems.'

'Kenneth didn't tell me he was married.'

'Maybe Kenneth didn't know.'

Angus thought about that and then nodded, understanding. 'Aye. Maybe he wouldn't. Rory learned early to keep things to himself where Kenneth was concerned.'

'But you'd like to see them?'

'I'd like to see them,' Angus agreed.

'Could you give them a bed for the night?' Jake asked—diffidently—and held his breath.

The old man considered. He stared through the window down at his garden—his vegetable patch, where Jake knew he was longing to be right now.

Since his illness he'd drawn in on himself. He barely tolerated the housekeeper being here. Could he accept strangers?

How much had he loved Rory?

Jake held his breath some more.

'Rory's widow,' Angus whispered at last. 'What would she be like?'

'I don't know,' Jake told him. 'I only met the sister. Kirsty. She seems…temperamental.'

'What does temperamental mean?'

'I guess it means she's cute,' Jake admitted, and Angus gave a crack of laughter that turned into a cough. But when he recovered there was still the glimmer of a smile remaining.

'Well, well. Signs of life. Time and enough, too. That wife of yours has been gone too long.'

'Angus…'

'I know. It's none of my business. You're saying these women are at the gate now?'

'Yes. I'll go and let them in if it's OK with you.'

'You think they should be staying here?'

'I think they should stay.'

Angus surveyed his doctor for long moment. 'She's cute?' he demanded, and he seemed almost teasing.

'Not Rory's wife,' Jake said stiffly. 'I've only met—'

'I know who you'd be talking about,' Angus said testily. 'Rory's wife's sister. She's cute?'

'Yes, but—'

'And if she's staying the night… You'll be back in the morning.'

'Yes, but—'

'Let's leave the buts,' Angus said, and his lined face creased into mischief. 'I'll not be flying in the face of providence. Cute, eh? Well, well. Of course they can stay.'

CHAPTER TWO

OK, so Angus was matchmaking but that was fine by him. Anything to get him to agree to have them stay, Jake decided as he made his way down the magnificently carved staircase.

He walked out the front door and stopped.

He'd left his car blocking the castle entrance, with only just enough room for a pedestrian to squeeze past. The verge on either side was rough, corrugated by recent rains.

He'd expected Kirsty and her sister to walk along the cobblestones.

What had happened was obvious. One of the women hadn't been able to walk.

Halfway along the walkway was a wheelchair, upturned. A woman was lying in the mud. Kirsty was bending over her.

Jake took one look and started to run.

She was Kirsty's sister. There was no doubting it. An identical twin? Maybe. The similarities were obvious but there were major differences. The girl lying in the mud was heavily pregnant. Her face was bleached white and a fine hairline scar ran across her forehead. She lay in the mud and her eyes were bleak and hopeless. Jake had seen eyes like this before, in terminally ill patients who were alone and who had nothing left to live for. To see this expression on such a young woman was shocking.

'Oh, Susie, I'm so sorry,' Kirsty was saying. She was

kneeling in the mud, sliding her hands under Susie's face to lift her clear. 'There was a rut. It was filled with water and I didn't realise how deep it was.'

'What's happening?' Jake knelt and automatically lifted the woman's wrist. 'You fell?'

'You really are smart,' Kirsty muttered, flashing him a look of fury. 'I tipped her out of the wheelchair. Susie, what hurts? Have you wrenched your back? Don't move.' She sounded terrified. One hand was supporting Susie's head; the other was holding her sister down.

Jake's fingers had found the pulse, automatically assessing.

'Did you hurt yourself in the fall?' he asked, and the young woman in the mud shook her head in mute misery.

'I'll live.' She put her hands out to push herself up, but Kirsty's expression of terror had Jake helping her hold her still.

'What do we have here?' He held the woman's shoulders, pressuring her not to move. 'Can you stay still until I know the facts?' He spoke gently but with quiet authority. 'I don't want you doing any more damage.'

'She suffered a crush fracture at T7 five months ago,' Kirsty told him in a voice that faltered with fear. 'Incomplete paraplegia but sensation's been returning.'

'I can walk,' Susie said, into the mud.

'On crutches on smooth ground,' Kirsty told Jake, still holding her twin still. 'But not for long. There's still leg weakness and some loss of sensation.'

'Let me get my bag.'

'I can get up,' Susie muttered, and Jake laid a hand on her cheek. A feather touch of reassurance.

'Humour me. I won't take long, but I need to be sure you're not going to do any more damage by moving.'

It took him seconds before he was back, kneeling before her, touching her wrist again. Her pulse was steadying. He glanced again at Kirsty. If he had to say which was the whiter face, his money was on Kirsty's. Such terror…

'I'm going to run my fingers along your spine,' he told Susie. 'I'd imagine you'd have had so many examinations in the last few months that you know exactly what you should feel and where. I want you to tell me if there's anything different. Anything at all.'

'We need help,' Kirsty snapped. 'We need immobility until we can get X-rays. I want a stretcher lift and transport to the nearest hospital.'

But Jake met her eyes and held. 'Your sister's break was five months ago,' he said softly. 'There should be almost complete bone healing by now.'

'You're not an orthopaedic surgeon.'

'No, but I do know what I'm doing. And it's soft mud.'

'Hooray for soft mud,' Susie muttered. 'And hooray for a doctor with sense. OK, Dr Whatever-Your-Name-Is, run your spinal check so I can get up.'

'Susie…' Kirsty said anxiously, but her sister grimaced.

'Shut up, Kirsty, and let the nice doctor do what he needs to do.'

'Yes, ma'am,' Jake said, and smiled.

So he did what he needed to do, while Kirsty sat back and alternatively glowered and leant forward as if she'd help and then went back to glowering again.

It was like two sides of a coin, he thought as he tested each vertebra in turn, lightly pressing, examining, running his fingers under Susie's sweater, not wanting to undress her and make her colder but finding he could examine by touch almost as easily as he could if she had been undressed. They had to be identical twins, he decided as he worked. One twin battered and pregnant. One twin immobilised by terror.

But Susie's spine was fine, he decided. Or as fine as it could be at this stage of recovery. As far as he could see, there was no additional damage.

There was still a complication. 'How pregnant are you?'

'Eight months,' she told him. 'Four weeks to go.'

'There's already been a false labour,' Kirsty muttered.

'So you decide to go travelling,' he said dryly. 'Very wise.'

'Mind your own business,' Kirsty snapped.

'Be nice,' Susie told her twin, and Kirsty looked surprised, as if she wasn't accustomed to her sister speaking for herself.

'You've flown from the US to Australia at eight months pregnant?' he asked Susie, but Susie didn't answer.

Kirsty waited for a moment to see if her twin would answer, but when she didn't, she spoke again. 'We came a month ago. We thought it might help Susie if she could find Rory's Uncle Angus and talk to him about Rory. But Susie went into prem. labour and it's taken a month before we've been game enough to leave Sydney. Enough of the inquisition. Could we get Susie warm, do you think?'

Kirsty's anger and distress were palpable. She'd have liked to direct them straight at him, Jake thought, but he could see the warring emotions on her face and knew that the anger and the distress were self-directed. She was blaming herself.

But he had to concentrate on Susie. Triage decreed that psychological distress came a poor second to possible spine damage. He was helping Susie into a sitting position, and now he smiled at her, encouraging.

'Slow. I don't want any sudden movements.'

'This doctor's almost as bossy as you are,' Susie told her sister. 'Nice.' She turned back to Jake. 'But be bossy with Kirsty,' she told him. 'She needs bossiness more than me.'

'I'll deal with your sister after you,' Jake told her, and glanced between the two of them. There was more going on here than a healing back and pregnancy. Why was Kirsty so terrified?

Susie was so thin.

'Is anything else hurting?'

'My pride,' Susie told him, and some of her bravado was fading. 'I have mud everywhere.'

'Can we take her inside?' Kirsty demanded in a voice full of strain, and Jake glanced at her again. OK. Enough of the mud.

He stooped and lifted Susie up into his arms. Despite her pregnancy, she was so light she alarmed him even more.

Kirsty gave a sigh of relief and started tugging the wheelchair forward, but instead of placing Susie into it he turned toward the gate.

'Hey,' Kirsty said. 'Put her in here.'

'The chair's wet,' he said reasonably. 'And we still have to get past the truck.'

'You can't carry her.'

'Why not?'

'You should say *Unhand my sister, sir,*' Susie told her sister, and Kirsty's eyes widened. She seemed totally unaccustomed to her sister even speaking, much less making a joke.

'My stupidity with the car blocked your path,' he told Kirsty, sending her a silent message of reassurance with his eyes. Relax, he was telling her. We need to get your sister warm. The least I can do is provide alternative transport.

And it seemed that finally she agreed with him.

'Well, if you think you can bear the weight...'

She was trying to smile, but he could still see the fear.

'We Aussie doctors are very strong,' he told her, striving to match her lightness, and at last she managed to smile. He liked it when she smiled, he decided. She had a great smile.

A killer smile.

'Australian doctors are trained in weightlifting?'

'Part of the training—just after learning where lungs are. But if you want to see strong... I have it on good authority that the man you're about to meet was an all-time champion cabertosser in his youth. Small but tough is our Lord Angus.'

'What's a caber?' Susie asked, bemused, and he grinned.

'Who knows? That's a Scottish secret. I'm not privy to such things. But just between you and me, I suspect it's some sort of medieval instrument. Probably made out of boar's testicles, meant for stirring porridge.'

And to the sound of Susie's chuckling—and Kirsty's gasp of amazement—he led one woman and carried another up the steps of Loganaich Castle.

He'd made her sister smile.

Kirsty helped Susie wash and undress, tucked her between sheets in the most sumptuous bed she'd ever seen and then stood back while Jake examined her. He examined her thoroughly, as if he had all the time in the world. The man who'd been in such a hurry a few minutes ago was acting now as if time was not important.

He made Susie laugh.

But as he did, he checked everything about her. Her heart rate, the baby's heart rate, the baby's position, her back. He examined the scarring. He checked sensation all over. He even found a set of bathroom scales and made Susie weigh herself. Normally an examination like this would have Susie climbing walls, but Susie tolerated it with equanimity and she even laughed some more.

She never laughed these days.

He told the best jokes, Kirsty thought as she stood well out of the way and watched the skilled way he drew Susie out. He made gentle cracks that you weren't sure were jokes—or not until you looked into his eyes and saw the lurking twinkle. He was just what Susie needed.

No, he was just what *she* needed, she thought gratefully as she watched him take over. For the first time in months the heavy responsibility for her sister's health had been shifted to someone else.

Maybe they could stay here for a while.

She hadn't even met Uncle Angus yet, she reminded herself. Their host. The earl.

'When did you last eat?' Jake was asking Susie, and Kirsty had to haul herself together to listen to what he was saying. He had

Susie tucked back into bed after the weighing. She was smiling up at him, and the sight of her smiling sister made Kirsty smile.

'When did you last eat?' Jake asked again, as she failed to answer, and Kirsty blinked and responded for her.

'Um… Lunchtime. Four or five hours ago.'

'What did you eat then, Susie?' he asked her sister, and Kirsty blinked again. He'd gone straight to the heart of the matter. He was some doctor!

'I had a sandwich,' Susie said, and Kirsty opened her mouth to say something but Jake glanced at her again. This man could speak with his eyes.

She shut up—as silently ordered.

'How much of the sandwich did you eat, Susie?'

'I…'

'I want the truth.' He was smiling but there was something about the way he said it that told Kirsty he already knew the truth.

'Half a sandwich,' Susie whispered, and then as Jake's eyes held hers—and held some more—she faltered. 'A quarter, maybe.'

'Is there a reason you're not eating?'

'Eating makes me feel sick.'

Kirsty was holding her breath. The world was holding its breath.

'Has that been happening ever since your husband was killed?'

They'd been tiptoeing round the edges for so long that this direct approach was almost shocking. Silence. Then… 'Yes.'

'Have you talked to a professional about your problems with eating?'

'Why should I talk to anyone about it?' Susie whispered. 'Kirsty keeps on and on…'

Kirsty opened her mouth but she was hit by that quelling glance again. *Shut up,* his glance said, and she wasn't going to argue.

'You don't see not eating as a problem?' he asked Susie.

'No.'

'Is that true? It's not a problem?'

'The only person who thinks it's a problem is Kirsty. And she fusses. It's just I don't feel like it.'

'I guess you don't feel like much.'

'You're right there,' Susie said bitterly. 'But people go on and on at me...'

No need for the quelling glance this time. Kirsty knew when to shut up. If she could, she'd disappear, she thought. He was treading on eggshells but she knew instinctively that none would be squashed.

'You know, Susie, I think you need time out,' Jake said softly. He glanced at the notes he'd been taking as he'd examined her. 'For a start, your blood pressure's higher than it should be and we need to get it down.'

'I'm not going to hospital.'

'I didn't suggest that,' he said evenly. 'But if you think you can bear to slum it here for a while...'

Susie gazed up at him from her massive eiderdown and her mound of soft down pillows. Astonished.

'Here?'

'You're Angus's family. I'm sure he'd be delighted to hold on to you for a week or so. I'll talk to him about it, shall I? But meanwhile you need to eat, and then sleep.'

'I'm not hungry.'

'You know, I'm very sure you are,' he told her. 'I cook the world's best omelette.'

'I don't understand,' Susie complained.

And Kirsty thought, Ditto.

'But you'll eat my omelette? I'll be hurt if you don't.'

How could her sister resist an appeal like that? Kirsty wondered. And if there was a tiny seed of bitterness in what she was thinking, who could blame her? Sure, persuade Susie to eat his omelette or she'd hurt his feelings. How many uneaten meals had she cooked for Susie?

She was being ridiculous. She looked up at Jake to find he was watching her, and the amusement was back behind those calm grey eyes. Drat the man—was he psychic? Could he read what she was thinking?

'I'll make some for your sister, too,' he told Susie, and Kirsty flushed.

'I'll make my own,' she told him. 'If Uncle Angus says I can. It is his castle after all. Isn't it?'

'It is indeed,' Jake said gravely. 'Susie, if you'll excuse us, I'll take your sister to meet him. We'll make your apologies. You can meet him in the morning.'

'What gives you the right…?' Kirsty was almost speechless but as soon as the door was closed against Susie's ears she found speech was close to overwhelming her. 'What gives you the right to invite Susie for an extended stay with a man she hasn't met? With an uncle who's dying? Are you his doctor or his keeper? Who are you? And weren't you late before?'

'I'm his doctor and his friend,' he said bluntly. He was striding down the hallway so fast that she had to almost break into a run to keep up with him. It seemed his time constraint—his sense of urgency—was operating again. 'We have it in our grasp to save three lives here, Dr McMahon, and in the face of that, who am I to quibble at being later than I already am?'

'I don't understand.'

'Susie, her baby and Angus,' he told her, wheeling into the next corridor. This mansion was vast, Kirsty thought as she struggled to keep up. It was astounding. It was furnished like a palace. Actually…

'It's not a very exclusive palace,' Jake commented. 'Louis XIV meets Discounts-R-Us.'

It was so much what she was thinking that she gasped.

'Angus's wife had grand ideas,' he told her, reaching the stairs and taking them three at a time. 'But by the time the mansion was built Angus said enough was enough. He's rich but he's not stupid. One day this place will be a glorious tourist hotel—the views alone are enough to sell it for millions. He didn't stint on the building, but furnishings to suit were another matter. So we have a fabulous ballroom with a magnificent but very plastic chandelier. Plus the rest.'

It was amazing—but it was great, Kirsty thought, looking around her in awe. There were aspidistra plants winding up every column—and there were many, many columns. Grecian columns. If she looked closely, she could see the plants were plastic. Made in China. The Louis XIV chairs scattered along the wall were of a construction about three classes below chain-store.

What was she doing, being distracted by furnishings? She was still annoyed. She decided to go back to being furious. But before she could resurrect her indignation, he let loose with his own.

'Do you mind telling me what you're doing, travelling the world with a woman who is eight months pregnant? A woman who has a shattered back and who's anorexic to boot? What madness propelled you to bring her halfway across the world? I'm not talking lightly when I say we're working on saving three lives. She's risking her life and her baby's life.'

'You think I don't know that? She would have died if I hadn't brought her here,' she said flatly. 'And there's the truth.'

'Why?'

'You can see why. She fell for Rory so hard she couldn't see anyone else, and when he was killed she wanted to die, too. I think she still does.'

'Is she being treated for depression?'

'She refuses. She can't take antidepressants because of the baby, if she'd take them—which she wouldn't. She won't talk about Rory. She just sits. I hoped that by bringing her here, where people knew Rory, she might break her silence.'

He reached the landing and said over his shoulder, 'You said she's a landscape gardener.'

'That's part of the problem,' Kirsty told him. 'Susie's not fit to work. She has nothing, so she sits and thinks of what she's lost.'

'She still has the baby,' Jake says. 'It's not altogether tragic.'

'That's easy to say,' Kirsty said, and he flashed her a look that she couldn't read.

'I'm sorry.'

'Where are we going?'

'To meet Angus.'

'You said he'd be asleep.'

'I'd said he'd gone to bed. There's a difference. He'll be waiting for us.'

'He's so ill he wouldn't come to find out what's happening?'

'He's a bit like Susie,' Jake said, his voice softening. 'He should be in a downstairs bedroom but he refuses. He refuses anything that might help. He just sits and waits.'

'How close is he to death?' she asked bluntly, and saw him wince. He really did care.

'Until you arrived, I'd have said it'd be a matter of weeks.' Suddenly he was slowing his stride, as if it was important that she hear what he had to say. 'Days even. Once he's in a nursing home I imagine he'll lose any last vestige of will to live. He lives for this place.'

'For this castle?'

There was a wry grin at that. 'No. Loganaich Castle gives him pleasure but, as amenable as he was to building it, this was his wife's baby. He doesn't love it. His vegetable garden, though, is a different matter. But now...' He hesitated.

'Now?' she prodded, and he seemed to think for a bit before continuing.

'Now we have a landscape gardener and a doctor on hand,' Jake said. 'Who knows what difference that could make?' He paused before a pair of vast oak doors, set with two plastic plaques. DEIRDRE LIVES HERE was engraved on a teddy-bear-embossed plastic plaque hanging on the left-hand door and ANGUS LIVES HERE was hung with decorative fishing lines on the right.

It was too much for Kirsty. She started laughing. Jake

swung the door wide, and she was laughing as she met the Earl of Loganaich.

Serious lung deterioration was difficult to disguise and Angus showed all the symptoms. He was seated at the window but he stood as they entered, a frail man who groped for his walking frame before taking a faltering step toward them. His breathing was shallow and rasping, and his lips had a faint blue tinge.

If he was my patient, I'd have him on oxygen, Kirsty thought, and caught a flash of grim amusement from Jake.

She wasn't going to look at him any more.

That was easy enough to arrange—for the moment. Angus was coming toward her, a quizzical smile on his wrinkled face.

'Here's my visitor,' he said, his obvious pleasure giving lie to Jake's declaration that he couldn't have visitors. 'But not…' His face clouded in disappointment. She'd held out her hand to greet him and he stared down at her bare ring finger. 'Not Rory's widow? Jake's made a mistake, hasn't he? Rory never married.'

'He did,' Kirsty told him, confused. Why hadn't Rory kept in touch with his family?

'But you're not…'

'My sister married your nephew,' she told him.

'And she's not here.'

'Susie's here, but she's ill herself,' Jake said softly. 'We've popped her into bed. She's exhausted.'

'She's ill?' This old man was anxious on her sister's behalf, Kirsty thought with more than a little incredulity as she listened to his laboured, painful breathing.

'My sister's looking forward to meeting you very much,' she told him. 'Jake seems to think it's OK for us to stay the night.'

'Of course it is.'

'We won't bother you. And we'll leave first thing in the morning.'

His face fell. 'So soon?'

'We don't want to disturb you.'

'No one wants to disturb me,' he snapped, so harshly that he made himself cough. 'Why didn't Rory tell me he was married? Why didn't Kenneth tell me Rory was married?'

Kirsty had no answers. She knew Rory had a brother, but she'd never met him. As far as she knew, there was a deep and abiding dislike that had been the major decision behind Rory's decision to emigrate.

'Maybe Susie knows more than I do,' she murmured. 'You can talk to her in the morning.' She cast an uncertain glance at Jake, and then looked back at Angus. His lips were still tinged blue and his distress was obvious. He was struggling to stand. As she turned back to him he staggered slightly. She caught his hand and helped him sit on the bed.

'Th— Th—' It was too much. He lay back on the pillows and gasped.

'You need oxygen,' she said urgently, and turned to Jake. 'Why isn't he on oxygen? It'd surely help.'

Jake sighed. 'Thank you, Dr McMahon. The US has heard of oxygen, then, has it?'

'I'm sorry,' she said, backing off in an instant. What was she about, interfering in a doctor-patient relationship that had nothing to do with her? 'Of course it's none of my business. And Angus—your… I'm sorry, I don't know what to call you.'

'I haven't done the introductions,' Jake said. 'Dr Kirsty McMahon, this is His Grace, the Earl of Loganaich.'

She glowered, and then shot a cautious smile at Angus. 'Gee, that makes it easier to know what to call you.'

Angus managed a smile back—and so did Jake.

'Call me Angus,' the old man managed. But then he started to gasp again and Jake's smile died.

'Angus, you need to let me help you,' Jake said urgently, and Kirsty could hear the raw anxiety in his tone. This was something much deeper than a doctor-patient relationship.

'Angus won't use oxygen,' Jake added, startling her by referring to a conversation she thought he'd effectively closed. 'I know it's none of your business, Dr McMahon, but now you've brought it up we may as well give Dr McMahon an answer, don't you think, Angus?'

'No,' Angus gasped, and struggled for some more breath.

'Angus won't use oxygen because he's decided to die,' Jake said, still roughly. 'Just like your sister. Just like Susie.'

'Susie wants to die?' Angus gasped. 'Rory's wife wants to die? Why?'

'The same reason you do, I expect,' Jake growled. 'No point in going on.' Then, as Angus started coughing again, he lifted the old man's hand and gripped, hard. 'Angus, let us help. Stop being so damned stubborn.'

Kirsty took a deep breath. She glanced sideways at Jake—and then decided, Dammit, she was going in, boots and all.

'You know, the way you're looking, without oxygen you could well die in the night,' Kirsty said softly. 'Susie's travelled half a world to meet you. She'd be so distressed.'

'I'm not… I'm not likely to die in the night.'

Kirsty cast another cautious glance at Jake but for some reason Jake had turned away. Go ahead, his body language said. This may be none of her business but he wasn't stopping her.

'Jake's told you I'm a doctor,' she said, and Angus took a couple more pain-racked breaths and grunted.

'Aye. Too many of the creatures.'

'He means two too many,' Jake said. He'd crossed to the window and was staring out at the sea. 'Until you arrived I was the only doctor within a hundred miles. Why he should say there's too many doctors when he won't even agree to see a specialist…'

'No point,' Angus gasped. 'I'm dying.'

'You are,' Kirsty said, almost cordially. 'But don't you think dying tonight when Susie's come all this way to see you might be just a touch selfish?'

There could have been a choking sound from the window, but she wasn't sure.

'Selfish?' Angus wheezed and leaned back on his pillows. 'I'm not… I'm not selfish.'

'If you let Dr Cameron give you oxygen then you'd certainly live till morning. You might well live for another year or more.'

'Leave me be, girl. I won't die tonight. No such luck.'

'Your lips are blue. That's a very bad sign.'

'What would you know?'

'I told you. I'm a doctor. I'm just as qualified as Dr Cameron.'

He gasped a bit more, but his attention was definitely caught. The veil of apathy had lifted and he seemed almost indignant. 'If my lips were blue then Jake would be telling me,' he managed.

'Jake's told you,' Jake muttered from his window, and glanced at his watch. And did his best to suppress a sigh. And went back to staring out the window.

There was a moment's silence while Angus fought for a retort. 'So my lips are blue,' he muttered at last. 'So what?'

Kirsty considered. Back home she worked in a hospice and she was accustomed to dealing with frail and frightened people. She could sense the fear in Angus behind the bravado.

Maybe he wasn't ready to die yet.

Another glance at Jake—but it seemed he was leaving this to her.

'Let us give you oxygen,' she said, wondering how she was suddenly taking over from an Australian doctor, with a patient she didn't know, on his territory—but Jake's body language said go right ahead. 'And let us give you some pain relief,' she added, guessing instinctively that if he was refusing oxygen, he'd also be refusing morphine. 'We can make a huge difference. Not only in how long you're likely to live but also in how you're feeling.'

'How can you be knowing that for sure?' he muttered.

'Angus, I have a patient back home in America,' she said softly. 'He's been on oxygen now for the last ten years. It's given him ten years he otherwise wouldn't have had—ten years where he's had fun.'

'What fun can you have if you're tied to an oxygen cylinder?'

'Plenty,' she said solidly. 'Cyril babysits his grandson. He gardens. He—'

'How can he garden?' Angus interrupted.

And Kirsty thought, Yes! Interest.

'He wheels his cylinder behind him wherever he goes,' she told him. 'He treats it just like a little shopping buggy. I've watched him weeding his garden. He used a kneepad 'cos his knees hurt, but he doesn't even think about the tiny oxygen tube in his nostril.'

'He's not like me.'

'Jake says you have pulmonary fibrosis. He's just like you.'

'I haven't got a grandson,' Angus said, backed into a corner and still fighting.

'No, but you'll have a grand-niece or -nephew in a few weeks,' she said with asperity. 'I do think it'd be a shame not to make the effort to meet him.'

The effect of her words was electric. Angus had been slumped on the bed, his entire body language betokening the end. Now he stiffened. He stared up at her, disbelief warring with hope. The whistling breathing stopped. The colour drained from his face and Kirsty thought maybe his breathing had totally stopped.

But just when she was getting worried, just when Jake took a step forward and she knew that he'd had the same thought as she had—heart attack or stroke—Angus started breathing again and faint colour returned to his face.

'A grand-nephew.' He stared up, disbelief warring with hope. 'Rory's baby?'

'Susie's certainly pregnant with Rory's child.'

'Kenneth would have said—'

'Kenneth—Rory's brother—doesn't want to know Susie,' Kirsty told him, trying to keep anger out of her voice. 'He's made it clear he wants nothing to do with us. So we came out here hoping that the Uncle Angus who Rory spoke of with af-

fection might show a little affection to Rory's child in return.'
She steadied then and thought about what to say next. And
decided. Sure, this wasn't her patient—this wasn't her
hospice—but she was going in anyway. 'And you can't show
affection by dying,' she told him bluntly. 'So if you have an
ounce of selflessness in you, you'll accept Dr Cameron's
oxygen—and maybe a dose of morphine in addition for
comfort—you'll say thank you very much, and you'll get a
good night's sleep so you can meet your new relative's mother
in the morning.'

But he wasn't going so far yet. He was still absorbing part
one. 'Rory's wife is pregnant.' It was an awed whisper.

'Yes.'

'And I need to live if I'm to be seeing the baby.'

'Yes.'

'You're not lying?'

'Why would she lie?' Jake demanded, wheeling back to the
bed. 'Angus, can I hook you up to this oxygen like the lady
doctor suggests, or can I not?'

Angus stared at him. He stared at Kirsty.

His old face crumpled.

'Yes,' he said. 'Yes, please.'

Jake had an oxygen canister and a nasal tube hooked up in
minutes. He gave Angus a shot of morphine and Angus
muttered about interfering doctors and interfering relatives
from America and submitted to both.

Within minutes his breathing had eased and his colour had
improved. They chatted for a little—more time while Kirsty
noticed Jake didn't so much as glance at his watch again—and
finally they watched in relief as his face lost its tension. He'd
been fighting for so long that he was exhausted.

'We'll leave you to sleep,' Jake told him, and the old man
smiled and closed his eyes.

'Thank God for that,' Jake said softly, and ushered Kirsty
out the door. 'A minor miracle. Verging on a major one.'

'You really care,' she said, and received a flash of anger for her pains.

'What do you think?'

There was only the matter of Susie's omelette remaining.

'I can do it,' Kirsty muttered as Jake led her down to the castle's cavernous kitchen. Somewhat to her relief, Deirdre's love of melodrama and kitsch hadn't permeated here. There was a sensible gas range, plus a neat little microwave. And a coffee-maker. A really good coffee-maker.

'I'm staying here for ever,' Kirsty told Jake the moment she saw it. She hadn't seen a decent coffee since Sydney. 'Dr Cameron, I can take over now. We'll be fine.'

'Call me Jake.' Boris had followed them into the kitchen. The man and his dog were searching the refrigerator with mutual interest. 'If you take your sister an omelette, will she eat it?' he demanded. She stopped being flippant and winced.

'Um…no.'

'How did I guess that? I'll take it.'

'But you have more house calls.'

'The girls will already be asleep,' he muttered. 'I may as well stay.'

'Your wife goes to bed early?' Kirsty asked, and he looked at her as if she was stupid. Which, seeing she was hugging a coffee-maker, might well be a reasonable assumption.

'Forget it,' he said. 'You. Toast. Me. Omelette.' And he grinned down at the hopeful Boris. 'And you—sit!'

'Fair delineation.'

'Speaking of delineation—you don't want a medical partnership, do you?' he asked, without much hope and from the depths of the refrigerator.

'You don't even know me,' she said, startled.

'I know you enough to offer you a job.'

'You can't be so desperate you'd offer a strange American a medical partnership.'

'I'm always desperate.' Backing out from the fridge with

supplies, he separated eggs and started whisking the whites as if they'd offended him.

Kirsty cast him a sideways glance—and decided his silence was wise. She'd be silent, too. She started making toast.

For a while the silence continued, but there was obviously thinking going on under the silence. Kirsty was practically exploding with questions but Jake exploded first.

'Where are you expecting Susie to have her baby?' he asked at last, and his voice held so much anger that she blinked. He'd moved on from offering partnerships, then. He was back to thinking she was a dodo.

'Sydney,' she told him. 'We've booked her into Sydney Central.'

'You mean you've thought it through.'

'I'm not dumb.'

'You've towed a wounded, damaged, pregnant, anorexic woman halfway round the world—'

'I told you. I had no choice. She was dying while I watched. Susie's my twin and I love her and I wasn't going to let that happen.'

'So what did you hope to achieve here?'

'Susie loved Rory so much. I thought she might just find echoes. And maybe she will yet,' she added a trifle defiantly, flipping the toast onto a plate. 'Angus's smile…when he smiles, it's Rory's smile.'

'He was very fond of Rory,' Jake said, relenting a little.

Maybe he'd been afraid she'd intended dumping Susie's pregnancy on him, she thought, and if she were a medical practitioner in such a place, maybe she'd be angry, too.

'That's what I'm hoping,' she said. 'You know, this castle is just the sort of crazy extravagant thing Rory might have built. Tell me about it.'

'It saved this district's soul,' Jake told her and she paused in mid-toast-buttering.

'Pardon?'

'This is a fishing town,' he said, flipping the omelette then moving in to remove her toast crusts with meticulous care. Boris moved in to take care of the waste. 'The town was dependent on 'couta. Fish,' he told her when she looked mystified. 'Nearly all the boats were designed to catch barracouta, but forty years ago the 'couta disappeared, almost overnight. The locals say there was some sort of sea-worm that decimated them. Anyway, the boats all had to be refitted to make them suitable for deeper sea fishing but, of course, no one had savings. The locals were desperate—half the town was living on welfare. Then along came Angus, Earl of Loganaich, and his eccentric, wonderful wife. They took one look at the place and decided to build their castle. The locals called it a crazy whim, but now, after knowing Angus for so long, I'd say it's far more likely he knew the only way to save the town was to give the locals a couple of years' steady income while they worked on their boats part time and regrouped.'

'You think that's what happened?'

'Who knows? But the locals won't have a word said against him. No one laughs at this castle. Do you think this'll do?'

She looked down at his plate. He'd cut two pieces of toast into perfectly formed triangles, without crusts. He'd flipped his perfect omelette into the centre.

'Whoops,' he said, and crossed to the back door. Seconds later he was back with one tiny sprig of parsley. It looked wonderful.

The man wasn't a doctor. He was a magician.

'Stay here,' he ordered. 'I need to feed my patient. You reckon she'll eat it?'

'I...um, I reckon,' she whispered. Her stomach rumbled.

'The rest is for you,' he told her, motioning to the remaining eggs. 'I'd do it for you, but I really am busy.'

'Sure,' she said, but he was already gone, striding toward the bedroom where Susie lay, not wanting to eat.

I'd eat, Kirsty thought, dazed. If Jake was standing over me having cooked me a meal...

How could she help but eat?

CHAPTER THREE

'HE'S gorgeous.'

Sitting on the end of her sister's bed, Kirsty knew exactly who she was talking about. Who else?

There was an empty plate on her bedside table. Susie had eaten everything. Two slices of toast and a two-egg omelette. Now she was cradling a cup of tea as if she was enjoying it.

'He is gorgeous,' Kirsty admitted, and smiled. 'Mind you, I can see that he'd put on a special effort when you're around. You're one glamorous widow.'

'Kirsty…'

'I know. I'm sorry.' Rory's death was still too new, too raw for her sister to even think that at some time in the future she might feel sexual attraction rekindled.

'No, but you,' Susie said thoughtfully. 'Kirsty, this is an extremely attractive male.'

'With a wife and daughter. Or daughters.'

'How do you know?'

'He said he had to get home to his girls.'

'Darn.' Susie finished her tea and snuggled further under the covers. Her toss out of the wheelchair seemed to have done her little harm, Kirsty thought. She looked brighter than she'd been for months. She looked interested. 'Angus is nice?'

'Angus seems lovely.'

'I thought he must be. Rory told me he was special. It was

only Kenneth being so awful that stopped him bringing me over
to meet him.'

'Why is Kenneth so awful?'

'I don't really know,' Susie said wearily. 'Rory seemed to
think he's mentally unstable. He made Rory's childhood miserable. Kenneth came over to America just before Rory died.
He came to the front door one night and he was just…weird.
Rory didn't let him stay. He took him out to dinner but he came
home so shaken… I thought then that Rory would never want
to return to Australia. The only good thing about Australia as
far as I could see was Rory's Uncle Angus and his Auntie
Deirdre. Do you suppose Angus really is an earl? Why do you
think Rory didn't tell me?'

'I have no idea,' Kirsty told her. 'Can I take your blood
pressure again before you go to sleep?'

'If you must. But it'll be down.'

It was, too, and by the time she'd checked it, Susie's eyes
were already closing.

'Do you think we might stay here for a while?' she asked
sleepily.

Kirsty thought, Why not? There was the little matter of her
medical career back home, but…well, maybe she had a medical
career right here.

She certainly had two patients, both of whom needed her.

As long they both shall live, she told herself fiercely. Please.

Kirsty found herself a bed in a bedroom that was just as sumptuous as Susie's. She set her alarm and checked her patients
twice during the night, but both were sound asleep and the
next morning she woke to find they'd decided to live a little
longer. She made them tea and toast, bullied them into eating
it, gave Angus more of the morphine Jake had left her, and then,
feeling like someone caught between sleep and waking—not
sure what was real and what was a dream—she showered in a
bathroom that had not only a chandelier hanging from the

ceiling but also had a vast oval portrait of Queen Victoria gazing sternly down on her nakedness.

She was just drying her toes and trying her hardest to ignore Her Majesty's displeasure when the doorbell rang. It was eight in the morning. Too early for casual visitors. It rang again two seconds later and she thought either Angus would try to go downstairs and open the door or Susie would go.

She had no choice. She wrapped her towel around her and ran.

Jake was at the door. And Boris.

'I thought you had a key,' she said, glowering, and he had the temerity to grin.

'Keys aren't half so much fun.'

She tried to slam the door but he shoved his foot through and walked in without so much as a by your leave.

'I could have used my key but I wasn't sure what sort of déshabillé I might find you in.'

'Yeah, I was swanning round naked.'

'Were you?' he asked with interest, and she flushed crimson.

'What do you think?' Then, as Boris nosed her towel, she backed sharply away. 'Can you keep your mutt back? This towel is precarious, to say the least.'

'Don't mind Boris,' he said, still smiling. 'You needn't think his intentions are dishonourable.'

'What is he?' she asked, momentarily distracted. He really was the strangest-looking mutt. Part bloodhound, part greyhound, part…ET? Huge droopy ears, a whippet-thin body and sad, protruding eyes that took over most of his weird-looking face.

'He's one of a kind,' Jake said, and Boris woofed in agreement, so enticingly she let go of one edge of the towel to scratch his ear. Very quickly she decided that wasn't a good idea. Both males were watching her towel—apparently with hope.

'You had him bred to your requirements?' she asked, and Jake gave a rueful and maybe even a resigned smile as she regained firm hold on her dignity.

'He's not my dog.'

'Sure he's not.' The dog was leaning against his leg, adoration oozing from every pore.

'Well, not for long,' he explained. 'Boris belonged to one of my patients. Miss Pritchard was the local schoolteacher, long retired by the time I knew her. She introduced me to Boris. I scratched his ear, just like you just did, and when she died six months ago that gesture had cost me a mention in her will. I told the public trustee there was a clause in the statutes saying doctors can't inherit from their patients, but the public trustee seemed to think Boris was an exception. No one would fight me for Boris.'

'You were fond of Miss Pritchard, as well as the dog,' Kirsty said slowly, working things out for herself, and now it was Jake's turn to look discomfited.

'Maybe. How are our patients?'

But the idea of his sort of country practice had her fascinated and she wasn't finished with questioning yet. Even dressed only in a towel. She might never get this chance again and she intended to use it.

'Were you born here?'

'No.'

'How long have you been practising here?'

'Four years?'

'Only four? Why on earth did you come?'

'I like it,' he said defensively.

'Sorry. Only asking.' She smiled down at Boris, who was sniffing her painted toenails with interest. 'How did your wife react when you turned up one day with Boris in tow?' she asked, and that was the end of the laughter. His smile died so fast she might well have imagined it.

'I need to get on,' he told her, glancing at his watch. 'I'll see Angus now. Would your sister like to see me as well?'

'I'd like you to see her,' she said frankly, abandoning Jake's past in the face of current medical need. 'To be honest…' She hesitated.

'To be honest, what?'

'When I came to Australia I thought I could look after her. But medically it's been a disaster. To be a loving sister and yet be a doctor as well…'

'You can't do the grumpy bits,' he said, softening slightly.

This was such a weirdly intimate setting. They were standing in the great hall, two Made-In-Japan suits of armour flanking the stairway behind them, Boris wagging his tail between them as if urging his master to hurry up—and Kirsty was standing in her bare feet with a two-foot width of towelling keeping her only just decent. Of course it was intimate. But Jake was now hardly noticing, Kirsty thought.

She should be grateful. She *was* grateful. But…

But what?

But nothing, she told herself crossly. Move on.

'I do the grumpy bits,' she said, and suddenly her voice was doing weird things, like she was having trouble finding a normal doctor-to-doctor tone. Well, what did she expect when talking to a colleague dressed like this? 'I tell her not eating will harm the baby. I tell her she has to be more optimistic, for the baby's sake if not her own.'

'Doesn't work, huh?'

'No,' she said frankly. 'And how can I blame her? I remember how lovely Rory was and I want to weep myself. How much worse must it be for Susie?'

'So no professional detachment.'

'None at all,' she said ruefully. 'Not one little bit. That's why I'm really pleased to see you.' She took a deep breath. 'Um…do you deliver babies?'

There was a lengthy pause. Maybe she should have gone and got dressed and talked about this on the way out, she thought, but there were a lot of decisions to be made here, and she suspected that many would be made in the next half-hour.

Would Angus keep his oxygen tube in place? Would he still be transported to the nursing home? If not, who would stay to take care of him? Maybe it could be her. But if so…that would mean that Susie stayed, too, and if she stayed then the baby would be born here and this man would have to deliver her. And—

'We're going too fast,' Jake said, and she blinked.

'Pardon?'

'Has Angus met Susie yet?'

'No. I thought—'

'Let's take this one step at a time, shall we?' he said, his smile a little wry. 'First things first. I've learned my triage, Dr McMahon, and I'm figuring out priorities. You know what I suggest you do first?'

'What?'

'Get yourself decent,' he told her. 'You have a very nice cleavage, and it's still just a cleavage but only just. That towel is way too skimpy. You're messing with my triage and making my priorities all wrong. So go cover priority number one with a T-shirt or similar while I find our patients. Then we can figure out what may or may not be more important than one scant inch of towelling.'

Dressed in record time, but still flushing bright crimson, Kirsty remerged from her gorgeous bedroom. There were voices coming from the room next to hers. Susie's room.

To her astonishment they were all in there. Susie was sitting up in bed, looking interested. Angus was seated in the armchair beside the bed. He was obviously still having breathing difficulties, but his colour was better than the night before. His nasal tube was taped in place and there was a small wheeled oxygen cylinder beside him. Like a tame pup.

The not-so-tame pup—Boris—was draped over the bed, looking adoringly up at Susie, and Susie was scratching his ears. Jake was beside the window.

They were all staring out the window to the garden beyond.

'He's not thriving,' Angus was saying in a voice that said the end of the world was nigh. 'I may as well go to that nursing home. If Spike dies…'

'Do we have another patient?' Kirsty asked, mystified, and they all turned to look at her.

'That's better,' Jake said, his eyes twinkling a little as he examined her demurely clad figure—but then he shook his head. 'Or maybe I just mean safer.'

She ignored him. Almost. 'Who's Spike?'

'Angus's pumpkin,' Susie said, and Kirsty blinked.

'Pardon?'

'He's a Queensland Blue,' Susie told her, as if that should explain all. 'Look at that veggie patch out there. Have you ever seen such a veggie patch?'

Kirsty crossed cautiously to the window and peered out, worrying that she had three demented patients on her hands. And a demented dog.

But it was indeed a veggie garden—and a veggie patch to take the breath away. It stretched over maybe a quarter of an acre, row upon row of vegetables and fruit trees of every imaginable variety with what looked like a conservatory on the side.

'Wow,' she said faintly.

'Wow's right.' Susie was pushing back her bedcovers—and pushing back Boris. 'I have to get out there.'

'You really think you can help?' Angus asked, and Susie gave him the sort of look Kirsty reserved for relatives of a patient who might well die. Huge sympathy and not wanting to encourage false hope.

'I'll do my best. We'll run soil tests. Maybe it's too damp. I'd imagine this rainfall's unseasonal for early in autumn. Is it?'

'Yes,' Angus said, with doubt. 'It's normally much drier.'

'Then maybe we can lift the whole vine—just enough to get it off the surface dirt and maybe get a bit of sunlight underneath. It can be done by thinning out the leaves. That should help the plant a lot. We need to be so careful. Dampness can cause rot this late in the growing season.'

'Rot,' Angus said in the voice of a parent hearing the word *leukaemia*, and Susie winced.

'I'm sorry. I don't want to scare you. But we need to get out there and see.'

'But you're pregnant, lass,' Angus said, looking at her with real concern. His old eyes misted with emotion. 'Pregnant with Rory's child.'

'And Rory wouldn't thank me if I just lay here while his Uncle Angus's pumpkin rotted,' she retorted. 'Kirsty, you have to help.'

'And you,' Angus said, turning and poking Jake in the midriff. 'You helped me come down to meet my new niece without so much as a jacket and Wellingtons. They're packed away in the back of my wardrobe. Get them for me, there's a good chap.'

'Yes, sir,' Jake said—and grinned.

Ten minutes later Jake and Kirsty were standing at the back door, onlookers to the main medical question of the day. Which was why Spike wasn't at his best.

The patient in question was a vast grey-green pumpkin. Susie was balancing on her crutches, trying not to wobble as she examined him from every angle, and Angus had pushed his oxygen cylinder onto its side so he could use it as a seat.

'Um…do we or do we not have a miracle happening here?' Jake asked, and Kirsty glared at him, as if by saying it he could jinx it.

'Don't even think it. Just hold your breath, hold your tongue and cross everything you possess.'

'Susie's weight-bearing is better than I thought.'

'I told you yesterday. She's weight-bearing but unsteady and she won't practise. The ground here's so soft and squishy, though, she's being forced to use her legs.'

'Praise be,' he said softly. 'And…you said Susie's a land-scape gardener?'

'That's right.'

'So Angus has a niece by marriage, pregnant with Rory's child, who shares his passion for gardening. A niece who needs accommodation for a few weeks.'

'You're going too fast,' she told him, and he raised his brows.

'Am I? Tell me you're not looking out at your sister and thinking this might work.'

'It's too soon to tell.'

'Yesterday you had a sister who was non-responsive and I had a patient who wanted to die. I don't see him refusing oxygen now.'

'He needs the tank for a garden seat,' she said, but grinned. 'OK, Dr Cameron, I concede you've done very well so far.'

'Most Australian doctors know enough to prescribe pumpkins for advanced pulmonary failure and severe depression,' he said, smiling in return. 'Hasn't that reached the States as standard practice yet?'

She choked on a bubble of laughter, and then looked out at Susie balancing precariously over the pumpkin but not even thinking about how wobbly her legs were, and thought, This is great. This could just work.

'Hey, Angus, I'd arranged to take you to the nursing home this morning,' Jake called, and the two pumpkin inspectors turned with identical expressions of confusion.

'Nursing home?' Angus said—and then he remembered and his face fell. 'Oh, aye. That's right.' He turned to Susie as if explaining. 'I agreed to go.'

'Why are you going to a nursing home?' Susie asked in astonishment, and he shook his head, defeat written all over him.

'It's time, lass. I can't keep on here. The doc is calling on me twice a day as it is, and he can't keep doing that indefinitely.'

'Angus has advanced pulmonary fibrosis,' Jake said gravely. 'He can't manage here alone any more.'

There was a moment's silence. 'Pulmonary fibrosis…does that mean you're dying?' Susie demanded, her already pale face blanching still further.

'It doesn't matter,' Angus said uneasily. 'We all go some time.'

'Not quite so soon as you're preparing to shuffle off,' Jake said bluntly. 'I've told you. With physiotherapy and with oxygen and pain relief you could still have years. Especially if you agree to bypass surgery.'

'I'll not be wanting years. What would I do with years?'

'You could grow bigger pumpkins,' Susie said wildly. 'Angus, I've only just met you. And you sound like my Rory. You're his uncle. If you die then I've got nobody.'

Gee, thanks very much, Kirsty thought, but she had enough sense to stay silent. And if she hadn't had enough sense, Jake's hand was suddenly on her arm, his pressure a warning. *I know*, she thought, annoyed, but then she glanced at his face and saw the tension and thought, This guy really cares.

Did he care about her sister? Maybe not, but he certainly cared for the old man. He was a country doctor in the old-fashioned sense, she thought, a man who knew every aspect of his patients' lives and who treated them holistically. Sure, he could set up an oxygen supply. He'd also plaster a broken leg or administer an antibiotic for an infection. But he looked at the whole picture, and he was looking at it now. Angus didn't need medicine as much as he needed family, and Jake was fighting with everything he had to give him one.

'Would you like us to stay?' Susie was asking Angus, and Kirsty held her breath. For Susie to make such a decision seemed amazing. Her twin had made no decisions since Rory had died. Even the decision of what to put on in the morning was beyond her. A crippling side-effect of depression was in-decision, and Susie had it in spades, yet here she was making an instantaneous decision all by herself.

Which might have to be revoked.

'We could only do that if Dr Cameron could deliver your baby,' she said tentatively, and Dr Cameron grimaced.

'I usually send my expectant mothers to Sydney two weeks before the birth.'

'Why?' Susie asked.

'A lone medical practitioner doesn't make for an ideal

birthing situation,' he told her. 'If you needed a Caesarean, I'd need an anaesthetist.'

Susie's face cleared. 'That's easy. Kirsty can give an anaesthetic. Not that I'll need it, mind. I intend to deliver this baby normally. Is that the only problem?' She turned again to Angus. 'Is it OK if we stay? We're stuck, you see. I came out to Australia to find you, but I was too close to my due date and now no airline will take me home. So if you need someone to stay here and I need somewhere to stay...we could really work on this pumpkin.'

Jake's hand was still on her arm, Kirsty realised. And he was looking at her. Angus and Susie had turned back to Spike the Pumpkin, and there was time to think things through before they took this plan any further.

How could she think when Jake's hand was on her arm?

She shook it off and he drew back, as if he hadn't meant to get so familiar.

Good. Or was it good?

'What's going on here?' Jake asked cautiously, glancing at her arm and then turning deliberately to look at Susie and Angus. 'This is happening so fast.'

'Susie's desperate for this.'

'I don't understand.'

'There was nothing,' Kirsty told him. He needed to see, she thought. She needed to make him understand the mess her sister was in. 'Rory was always really ambivalent about his background. He said he'd never got on with his parents and we knew his brother hated him. He arrived in America wanting to make a clean break and he did that by not talking about his background. The only person he ever mentioned was his Uncle Angus and that was only in passing—he'd never talk at length about him, and when Susie suggested maybe they come out here he was horrified. It was as if he'd decided that Susie was his family from now on, and that was that. Only then he died, and there was nothing. Just a blank nothing. Because there was no one else to grieve over him, it was almost as if Rory hadn't existed. And now Susie's found Rory's Uncle Angus, and he's lovely and he needs her and I'll bet right now she'll be thinking that Rory would want her to stay, and you can't imagine how much of a blessing that must be.' She broke off, tears threatening to spill. She wiped them away with an angry backhand swipe. 'Anyway, you've done very well.'

'For an Australian doctor,' he said with a hint of teasing, and she flushed and swiped again.

'I'm not crying,' she said. 'I don't cry. It's just…'

'Hayfever,' he said promptly. 'Caused by pumpkins. Can I prescribe an antihistamine?'

'I'm fine,' she said, and gazed at Susie some more. Susie had abandoned the crutches and was seated on the rock wall abutting the vegetable garden. She was talking animatedly about manure. Angus was listening and nodding and asking questions.

There were a few things to be considered. Medical things. It was up to her to consider them.

'Can we deliver Susie's baby here?'

'It's not perfect,' he told her. 'Normally I'd say no. But if we're weighting up the pros and cons, I'd say the pros definitely outweigh the added cons. Wouldn't you say so, Dr McMahon?'

'Maybe.'

'What sort of a doctor are you?'

'An American one,' she snapped, and he grinned.

'Yeah, and a cute one. But don't you guys all have specialties?'

'I guess.' She looked at him speculatively. 'You're a family doctor.'

'A generalist,' he agreed. 'But with surgical training.'

'Do you have an anaesthetist?'

'Not now. Old Joe Gordon was an anaesthetist—a fine one—but he died on me six months ago.'

'Which explains the overwork.'

'Which explains the overwork. So how about you?'

'I work in a hospice. A big one.'

'You're a palliative-care physician.'

'Um…no.'

'No?'

'My basic training's in anaesthesia,' she confessed. 'I specialise in pain management, hence the hospice work. You want a spinal block, I'm your man.'

His face stilled. His eyes turned blank. She could see cogs start to whirr.

'Let's not get any ideas,' she said hastily. 'I'm here to look after my sister.'

'How interested are you in pumpkins?'

She glanced across at the bent heads and managed a smile.

'Not very,' she confessed. 'They lack a little in the patient backchat department.'

'Then maybe you'd help me out?'

'How can I do that?' She was still watching her sister. Susie was sitting on the wall with Angus. The sun was on her face and she and Angus were examining each pumpkin leaf in turn. 'I need to be here with Susie. And with Angus. You said yourself that Angus couldn't be left alone. Ditto Susie. So that leaves me…'

'Stuck in a castle,' he said, still smiling, and she wished suddenly that he wouldn't.

'I guess that's terrific,' she said, with what she hoped was cheerfulness. It didn't quite come out that way. She looked dubiously across at her sister and realised that Susie and Angus were soul mates. They'd spend what remained of Susie's pregnancy happily saving pumpkins.

Maybe she could…um…read some books.

'Maybe you could help me,' Jake said again, and she turned from watching Susie and made herself concentrate.

'How could I do that?'

'I'm desperate.'

'You don't look desperate.'

He smiled. 'I have a way of hiding my desperation with insouciance.'

'Insouciance, hey? Like ketchup but thicker.'

His smile deepened. She loved it when he smiled like that. It made his eyes light up in a way that had her fascinated.

Remember Robert, she told herself fiercely. Remember her parents, Rory, a life committed to medicine.

Plus remember that this man was married. With kids. His girls…

'So exactly how desperate are you?' she tried cautiously, and his smile faded a little, as if he was weighing what he ought to tell her.

'Pretty desperate.'

'I can look after Angus.'

'He needs a nurse here,' Jake said slowly. 'But I was thinking…'

'Wow. Can I watch?'

The smile appeared again. A truly excellent smile. Well worth working for.

'Enough impertinence. I have an idea.'

'Another!'

'Shut up, you.' He was grinning. There'd been lines of strain around his eyes since the first time she'd met him, and suddenly they were lightening. It made her feel good. Great even. She found she was grinning back, and she had to force herself to get back to the issue at hand.

'Tell me your idea.'

'My girls…' he said cautiously, and she stopped feeling like smiling. Which was dopey. How could she be jealous of the family of someone she'd known for less than twenty-four hours?

'Tell me about your girls,' she managed.

'I have a housekeeper.'

'That's nice,' she said cautiously, and once again got that flash of laughter.

'It is nice,' he told her. 'But it gets nicer. Margie Boyce is a trained nurse. She's in her sixties but she's very competent. She could come out here during the day and stay with Angus and Susie.'

There were things here she wasn't quite understanding. 'You can manage without her?'

'No, but—'

'What about your girls?'

'That's just it,' he said patiently. 'They could come, too.'

'Your girls could come here?'

'That's right.'

'What about your wife?'

He sighed. 'I don't have a wife.'

There was a moment's silence. 'No wife.'

'No.'

'But girls.'

'You really are nosy.'

'I am,' she agreed, and beamed.

Her smile seemed to take him aback. He dug his hands in his pockets and stared at her like he wasn't quite sure what to make of her.

She continued to smile, waiting.

Hospice work was a hard training ground, Kirsty thought reflectively. She'd spent the last few years working with terminally ill patients, and one thing she'd learned fast was not to mess around trying to find the right way to frame a question. The people she worked with had little energy and less time. She worked to get things as right for them as she could in the little time she had available, and she didn't do it by pussyfooting around hard questions.

So maybe it made her nosy. What did she have to lose?

'I'm divorced,' Jake said grudgingly.

She gave a grunt of what might be sympathy and went back to looking out at the garden. That was another trick she'd learned. Give people space.

'So the girls are your daughters?' she asked at last.

'That's right.'

'How old?'

'Four.'

'Both?'

'They're twins.'

'Twins are great,' she said, and smiled.

He gave her a sideways look. Hmm. She stopped smiling, looking away, and he dug his hands deeper into his pockets. She thought that was the end of information but instead he started speaking again, carefully, as if explaining something distasteful.

'Laurel and I met at med school,' he said flatly, as if he wasn't sure whether he should be saying it, but now he'd started he wanted to get it over with fast. 'I became a surgeon, she was a radiologist, and I'm not even sure why we married now. I'm guessing we were too busy with our careers to look at anyone else. We were both hugely ambitious—fast movers in the career stakes—and our eventual marriage seemed more an excuse for a party than anything else. A party where we asked the right people. But suddenly Laurel was pregnant.'

'Not planned?' she queried gently, and he winced.

'Of course not planned. As far as Laurel was concerned, it was a disaster. She only agreed to continue the pregnancy on the understanding that we'd use childcare from day one.' He hesitated. 'And maybe I agreed with her. I was an only child with no concept of babies. But then…then Alice and Penelope were born.'

'And became people,' she said gently.

He looked surprised, as if he hadn't expected such understanding. 'I fell for them,' he conceded. 'My girls. But the reality of life with twins appalled Laurel. She hated everything about our new life, and she hated what the twins were doing to me. She issued an ultimatum—that we get a live-in nanny or she'd leave. That I return to the life we had pre-kids. So I was forced to choose. Laurel or the twins. But, of course, she knew my response even before she ever issued the ultimatum. The girls are just…too important to abandon to someone else's full-time care. So that was the end of our marriage. Laurel took off overseas with a neurosurgeon when the twins were six months old and she hasn't been back. So much for marriage.'

Ouch. That almost deserved being up there with other life lessons, Kirsty thought. All the reasons why it was dumb to get involved.

'So what did you do?' she probed gently.

'I moved to the country,' he said, almost defiantly. 'My career in Sydney was high-powered. I knew I'd see little of the twins if I stayed there and I had some romantic notion that life as a country doctor would leave me heaps of time with the kids. Pull a few hayseeds from ears, admire the cows, play with my babies…'

'It hasn't worked out quite like that, huh?'

'Well, no. But the problem is that I love it. The people are great. Alice and Penelope are loved by the whole community. They might not have as much of me as I'd hoped, but they have huge compensations.'

'And you? Do you have compensations?'

'Now we're getting too personal,' he said, stiffening as if she'd suddenly propositioned him. 'I don't do personal. The only reason I'm telling you this is because of Margie Boyce. As I said, Margie's a housekeeper-cum-nurse. She also acts as my baby-sitter. She's married to Ben, who was a gardener here before his arthritis got bad. Ben and Angus are old friends. What I've suggested to Angus in the past is that he has Margie and Ben stay with him, but of course he won't agree. He knows Margie looks after my girls so I'd need to find someone else, and the thought of Margie fussing over him when he wants to die is unbearable. But now…' Jake looked thoughtfully over to the two heads discussing pumpkins. 'If we tell Angus that a condition of Susie staying here is that Margie comes out to care for her during the day…bringing the girls with him… He may well agree.'

She thought that through. It sounded OK. 'That'd leave me doing nothing,' she said slowly.

'That'd leave you working with me,' he said bluntly, and gave her a sheepish smile. 'I've nobly worked it all out to stop you being bored.'

She tried to look indignant—and failed. She needed to be honest, she decided. She'd been kicking her heels in Sydney for the last month, waiting to see whether Susie went into premature labour, and by the end of that time she'd been climbing walls. Dolphin Bay was a tiny coastal village, and exploration would here be limited. She'd be bored to snores here, too.

'I don't think I can work here,' she said cautiously. 'Don't I need registration and medical insurance and stuff?'

'This is classified as a remote community. Really remote. That means the government is grateful for whoever it can get.' He glanced at his watch. 'It's still late afternoon yesterday in the States. If you give me a list of your qualifications and a contact number for the hospital you've been working in, I can get you accreditation to work right now. As in *right now*!'

'You really want me,' she said, awed, and he grinned.

'I really want you.' Then he hesitated. 'As a doctor.'

'Of course,' she said demurely. 'What else would you mean? But…to bring everyone here… What will Angus say to that?'

'I'll give it to Angus as a fait accompli,' Jake told her. 'You intend to work with me. He wants Susie to stay here, but Susie can't stay unless Margie stays here with her. Margie can't stay here unless the twins come, too, and Ben as well.

'This place has been like a tomb,' Jake went on, his smile disappearing as he tried to make her see how seriously he'd really thought this through. 'Since Deirdre died, Angus has locked himself away and waited to die as well. But he has so much to live for, if only he can see it. If I can throw open the doors, bring in his old friend, Ben, Margie to care for him, the twins to fill the castle with giggles and play-dough—and Susie and a new little baby to give him family again… Don't you think that might equal any anti-depressant, Dr McMahon? For Susie as well as Angus? What do you think?'

He was anxious, she thought incredulously. He was watching her and there was much more than a trace of anxiety behind the smile. He was waiting for her approval.

He didn't have to wait, she thought, throwing any remaining caution to the wind.

She was going into country practice.

He had her approval in spades.

CHAPTER FOUR

AT TWO that afternoon Kirsty was sitting beside Jake on her way to her first house-call, feeling bulldozed.

Back at the castle were Susie, Angus, Ben and Margie Boyce, Alice, Penelope and Boris. Maybe they were feeling equally bulldozed, but they certainly seemed happy. Susie and Angus had gone reluctantly to have an afternoon nap. Margie Boyce was baking. Jake's freckled and pigtailed four-year-olds were waiting to lick bowls, Boris was under the kitchen table, waiting for things to drop, and Ben was having a quiet dig in Angus's parsnip patch.

'How long did it take to work all that out?' Kirsty demanded, and Jake gave a self-satisfied smile and turned his car onto a dirt track leading away from the town.

'I work fast when I see rewards in front of me. Pretty good, huh?'

'Pretty fantastic,' she whispered. From the dark and gloomy castle of last night, there was now life and laughter and the chaos of a family. Even if it lasted only a day, this was worth it. Susie had been so bemused this morning she'd laughed at least half a dozen times, and that was six times more than she'd laughed since Rory had been killed. She thought the twins were great. They'd all sat at the kitchen table and eaten cold meat and salad for lunch, and Susie had hardly seemed to notice that she was eating.

The twins, two chirpy imps with their daddy's gorgeous

brown curls and eyes that were wide with innocence and mischief, hadn't permitted a moment's silence, and who could be desolate when they were around?

'It's excellent,' Jake said, and she grinned her agreement. But...

'There's no need to get too smug. If we come home and Boris has dug up the pumpkin patch...'

'Boris is a dog of intelligence,' Jake said solidly. 'Besides, it's a pumpkin patch. Now, if it was lamb shanks or even strawberries, I'd worry.'

There was a long contented silence. It wasn't just Susie and Angus who were benefiting from this, Kirsty thought. Her own mood had lightened about a thousand per cent.

And maybe some of that was to do with sitting beside Jake Cameron?

'Tell me about the patient you're taking me to see,' she said hurriedly, in an attempt to distract herself from thoughts she had no right to think. But she was thinking anyway.

For a moment she didn't think he'd answer. Maybe he was distracted too, she thought hopefully. Maybe he was thinking...

Cut it out!

'Mavis Hipton is a sweetheart,' he said softly, and she knew she'd been misjudging him. His face said all his attention was on his patient, and he was worried. 'She's eighty and has terminal cancer. Uterine cancer with bone metastases. Like Angus, she refuses to go into hospital. She's better off than Angus, though, in that she has her daughter caring for her. Barbara is looking after her mother really well.'

'So why do you need me to see her?'

'She has breakthrough pain. I can't keep it under control without making her so drowsy she can't read to her grandchildren. I saw her when I left you last night. I upped her morphine, but I was hoping you might be able to give me a more imaginative solution to the problem. I can ring a physician in Sydney to get advice, but without seeing her he's not much use. And...' He hesitated.

'And?'

'And he seems to think sleeping into death is the way to go,' Jake said bleakly. 'I'm hoping you disagree. Mavis may have a few months left, and if I can give her some quality time with her family...well, I'm damned if I'll deprive her of it unless I have to.'

Their destination was as far from Kirsty's Manhattan hospice as she could imagine. It was a tiny weatherboard shack, ramshackle around the edges but with bright gingham curtains in the window, hens clucking around what was obviously a well-tended garden and a toddler making mud pies on the front step. The lady who greeted them was wearing jeans, an over-sized shirt and big workman's boots. She was wiping her hands on a dishcloth as she opened the door, and she tossed the cloth aside to seize Jake's hands in welcome.

'Jake. I didn't think you'd make it back today.'

'I told you I would, Barbara.'

'Yeah, but you squeezed us in last night and we know how busy you are.'

'How did she sleep?'

'Like a baby,' Barbara told him. 'It was great that you did come. She was in so much pain.'

'And today?'

Barbara's eyes clouded. 'It's probably worse than it ought to be. She won't take any more of the morphine. She'll take it tonight, she says, but not now. It makes her drowsy and she says if she's going to sleep all the time then she may as well die right now.'

Jake grimaced. 'Maybe we can do better than that. Barbara, this is Dr McMahon. Kirsty's a pain specialist from the US. I wondered if your mum would mind seeing her.'

'Mum's delighted to see anyone,' Barbara said. She motioned to a bigger house along the track. 'That's where my hubby and I live,' she told Kirsty. 'But Mum gets lonely and her oven's better than mine. I've got scones in the oven right now. You go in and see her and by the time you finish I'll have the scones ready.'

'Who needs payment when we have scones?' Jake said lightly, bending down to admire the toddler's mud pies.

Kirsty's astonishment grew. Jake Cameron was a doctor with heart, she decided. Real heart. Most of the doctors she knew cared about their patients, but they'd not spare the time to stoop to admire a small child's mud pie—or to give their patient's daughter a swift hug, as Jake did as he passed Barbara to enter the house. Barbara sounded cheerful but her eyes were strained and bleak. Kirsty knew from experience that there was often little sleep for the primary caregiver. Not much sleep and too much heartache.

Mavis's bedroom was lovely. It was simply furnished, with an old double bed on a plain wooden floor, a worn rug and a vast patchwork eiderdown that was the centrepiece of the room. But it was the window that made it. From where the diminutive old lady lay, Mavis could see out over the veranda. She could see her granddaughter making her mud pies. She could see the hens scratching among the rose bushes, and in the distance she'd see the cows ambling lazily up toward the dairy from the clifftops further away.

Who would choose to be ill in hospital when you could be ill here? Kirsty thought, stunned. No one.

But the lady herself was in trouble. The look in Mavis's eyes suggested fear and pain. Relentless pain, Kirsty thought. She'd seen that look so many times. Acceptance that pain would be with her until the end.

A bottle of morphine mixture stood on the bedside table. Any time she wanted she could use this, Kirsty thought, appreciating that Jake had ensured Mavis could ease her pain whenever she wanted and drift into painless sleep. But she was obviously choosing not to.

Sleeping into oblivion had a distinct downside when there was so much life just through this window.

'So you're a pain specialist,' Mavis said as she walked in, and Kirsty realised she must be tuned in to everything that was said in the outer rooms. She'd be aching to be a part of the world again.

'Hello, Mrs Hipton,' she said, taking the lady's proffered hand. It was dry to touch—was she dehydrated? 'I'm Dr McMahon.' She hesitated, then added, 'Call me Kirsty.' That was something she'd never do back home. The use of first names in her Manhattan hospice was frowned on by the powers that be, but here it felt right.

'Where do you fit in?' Mavis whispered, and Kirsty saw it was an effort to talk. 'Don't tell me you flew in all the way from the States just to give me a consultation.'

'Kirsty's sister was married to Rory Douglas,' Jake told her, and the lady's eyes lit up with interest.

'Married to Rory. Angus's Rory?'

'My sister's visiting Angus,' Kirsty told her. 'So I thought I'd make myself useful while they get to know each other.'

'So Angus has family again,' Mavis breathed. 'Well, well. Isn't that lovely?' She managed a tight, pain-filled smile. 'Everyone should have family,' she whispered. Her sharp, intelligent eyes moved from Kirsty to Jake and back again. Questioning without words. 'Even Dr Cameron.'

'I think twins are enough family for anyone,' Kirsty said lightly, ignoring the innuendo. 'Mrs Hipton—'

'Call me Mavis.'

'Mavis, then.' Kirsty smiled. 'Could you bear it if you and Dr—if you and Jake gave me a complete history of your pain?'

Kirsty listened. For a while she didn't comment. She waited while Jake completed his normal examination. She sat while Jake talked, while he checked a pressure sore on Mavis's back, while he listened while Mavis told him about her granddaughter's attempt to conquer a tricycle. Jake was deliberately giving her space to think.

So she thought.

'I think I may be able to help a little,' she said at last, tentatively. 'That is, if you trust me.'

'I've checked Dr McMahon's credentials,' Jake told Mavis before the old lady could respond. 'She's the best.'

She shot him a surprised but gratified look. That was a compliment that must have come via her boss back home, but hearing it from Jake felt good.

'When did you last have morphine?' she asked.

'About four this morning.'

'Why not since?'

'I didn't need it.'

'You're hurting now. A lot.'

'I can bear it,' Mavis said. 'I thought… You get used to it. You get addicted to that stuff so it's not effective. If it gets really bad…'

'It's bad now,' Jake said gently, and Mavis flashed him a look of fear.

'I'm not dying yet.'

That was always the unspoken terror, Kirsty thought. That the pain would get worse and worse, and then when you needed it most the drugs wouldn't work.

'No,' Kirsty said softly, and she lifted Mavis's hand and held. 'You're not dying yet. But you are in pain. You know, morphine is an odd drug. If you take it to forget your troubles, as many addicts do, then, yes, you'll become addicted. It'll lose effectiveness and you'll need increasing doses. But if you have real pain—as you have—then it never loses its effect. I promise you. Mavis, I'm thinking you're suffering a lot of unnecessary pain because you're frightened of becoming addicted and because it's making you drowsy. Because of your fears, you're not taking the morphine regularly, which means you're getting a lot of pain before you take the next dose. You reach the stage where the pain's unbearable and then you finally take it. That's right, isn't it?'

'I… Yes,' she muttered, and Jake said nothing.

'Mavis, I promise you that morphine is *not* addictive if we use it in the right dose for the pain you're having. I promise you also that it will stay being effective for as long as you need it. What we need to do is to find the right dose. The dose is different for everybody, because everybody's pain is different. You need to start off by taking a prescribed dose of this mixture regularly every four hours. Slightly less than you're taking now—but regularly. I want you to promise me that you'll take this dose regardless. After a day or so the sleepiness will ease. The dose I'm prescribing will leave you free to enjoy life. It'll be regular and it'll keep the pain level tolerable. If, despite this, you have breakthrough pain, then I want you to take more, but I want the background dose to stay constant. I want you to call me every day, and we'll gradually increase the background dose until the pain is completely gone. Completely. And it will happen, Mavis. I promise. Then I'll change you over to a really convenient long-acting tablet that you can take just twice a day. That way we'll stay one step ahead of the pain, and you should rarely need to take the mixture. We're aiming to get rid of the pain completely—not just aim for good enough. We're aiming to get you out on the veranda, back into the kitchen when you're feeling well enough—not just watching life through a window.'

'But the morphine makes me so drowsy,' Mavis whispered. 'I don't want that. I have so little time. I can't just sleep....'

'Drowsiness often happens if you take a little too much occasionally,' Kirsty told her. 'You're waiting so long that you need a big dose to fight the pain and so you'll go to sleep. What we need to do is give you a little and often. Drowsiness is much less likely to happen then.' She smiled. 'And this is only step one. If morphine still makes you sleepy, we'll ditch it and try another drug. No excuses, Mavis. We need to get rid of this pain completely. Will you work with me to do that?'

Mavis glanced at Jake. Jake was smiling.

She looked back at Kirsty.

'You're staying for a while?'

'My sister's expecting a baby in a month. I'm not going anywhere.'

'So our Dr Jake has a partner for a month.'

'I guess he does,' Kirsty said. 'And you have a very bossy palliative-care physician. If you'll have me.'

'Jake doesn't mind?'

'Jake doesn't mind,' Jake said solidly from behind them. 'Kirsty looks like being a gift horse, Mavis, and I'm not one for looking gift horses in the mouth.

'Me either,' Mavis said soundly. 'Welcome to Dolphin Bay, love. I'd very much appreciate it if you could make me more comfortable.'

'Good,' Kirsty said cheerfully. 'Great.' She beamed at her patient. This sort of case was the reason she'd decided on her specialty. She'd missed her work so much, and to be useful again was wonderful. 'I'll have you bouncing in no time,' she told Mavis. 'But meanwhile you need to answer the question that every palliative-care physician worth her salt asks every patient.'

'Which is?'

'What's happening with your bowels?'

'That was fantastic.' Jake turned the car homewards and shot Kirsty a look of appraisal that was more than tinged with approval. 'Really great.'

'We don't know yet whether she'll follow instructions.'

'She'll follow instructions,' he said bluntly. 'Why wouldn't she? She's been in so much trouble that she wanted to die as soon as she could—and what I was doing wasn't helping.'

'You were keeping her pain-free. Or giving her the choice to be pain-free.'

'By doping her to the eyeballs.' His fingers clenched round the steering-wheel, so hard they showed white. 'There's so much I don't know in this job,' he said grimly. 'I barely touch the surface, and there's so much more. You have this information at your fingertips.'

'Caring for terminally ill patients is what I do every day of my working life. Of course I know my stuff. But I'd imagine my general medicine is a whole lot more limited than yours. Give me a good dose of chickenpox, and I'll run a mile.'

He grinned at that. 'Anyone in their senses would run a mile from a good dose of chickenpox.'

She chuckled. This felt good, she thought. More. It felt great. She could work with this man. She could even enjoy herself. For the next month…

'Would you be prepared to give an anaesthetic for minor surgery?' he asked, almost as if he was echoing her thoughts about them working together.

She nodded. 'Sure. Um…what needs doing?'

'I have a middle-aged farmer with a hernia who's desperate for an operation,' he told her. 'Francis is almost totally incapacitated by a hernia in his groin, but he's scared silly of city hospitals. He has it in his head that if he leaves here he won't come back. So he puts up with a hernia that makes him an invalid. For nothing. With a competent anaesthetist I could fix it in my sleep. If you're here…'

'You may as well make use of me, huh?'

'That's what I intend.'

Silence. Contented silence. Jake flicked the radio on, and something soft and happy drifted over the airwaves. On Kirsty's left was the sea, glistening sapphire, broken only by a battered blue fishing boat chugging ponderously back to harbour.

'This is heaven,' she whispered, and Jake glanced at her with a strange look.

'As you say.'

'It really would be a fantastic place to bring up kids.'

'That's why I'm here.'

She hesitated. They were nearing the castle now, and the car was slowing. 'What do you intend doing now?'

'This afternoon?'

'Yes.'

'Dropping you at the castle, collecting the Boyces, the twins and Boris and taking them all home,' he said promptly.

'But you have more work to do.'

'Yes, but you'll be back at the castle to take care of Angus and Susie, so there'll be no need for Margie to stay. Margie will take care of everyone back at the hospital residence.'

'You live in the hospital residence?'

'Yes.'

'Would you like to leave everyone at the castle for the rest of the afternoon?' she said impulsively, thinking of the pile of food she'd seen in Angus's freezer. 'Come back when you've finished work for the day and I'll cook you all dinner.'

His face stilled.

'No,' he said brusquely. 'Thank you.'

She stared. His tone had changed so dramatically that she was reminded of their first conversation, when he'd thought she and Susie were here after money.

'What have I said wrong?'

'Nothing.'

'Wouldn't you like to have dinner with m— with us?'

There was a moment's hesitation. 'Kirsty, I may as well say this straight out,' he said bluntly. 'It might sound dumb to state this so early, but I don't want you getting the wrong idea. I don't have relationships with women. My twins need all my attention and I can't mess them around.'

Silence.

More silence.

Her jaw seemed to hit her ankles. Lower. As a statement it was as effective as a wash of cold water, seemingly just as shocking.

'You don't have relationships with women?' Kirsty said at last, carefully, as if not trusting her voice. She didn't trust her voice.

'The twins and I manage very well by ourselves,' he told her. 'I've made a resolution not to mess with their lives by getting involved. I'm a dad first and foremost. Then I'm doctor to this district. My sex life comes a sad last.'

Her jaw dropped a bit more. Count to ten, she told herself fiercely. One, two…

She didn't make it.

'You don't have relationships with women,' she repeated, and he'd be a dope if he hadn't heard the anger surging in her voice. They'd arrived at the castle gates. He'd drawn to a halt and hit the remote that had the gates swing open. But he had to stop while they opened. 'What exactly do you mean by relationships?' she asked.

'You know.'

'I don't know,' she snarled. 'I've been working with you for the last hour. Does that define a relationship?'

'No, I—'

'I've been talking to you. I've been daring to impose on your personal space by making you talk back. You even smiled a couple of times. Does that constitute a relationship?'

'You know very well what I mean.' He looked flustered.

She thought, Good!

'So you're scared of coming to dinner with me and my sister and Angus and the twins and the Boyces and Boris. You're scared because that'll cause what you call a relationship. You're terrified that halfway through pudding I'll jump over the dining table and rip your clothes off.'

'Don't be—'

'Melodramatic?' she flung at him. 'Of course I won't be melodramatic. Don't you think it's you who's being just the faintest bit melodramatic, deciding that a casual invitation to you means I'm after your body? And don't you think that you're being just the tiniest bit insulting? You know nothing about me, Dr Cameron. For all you know, I may have a husband and six kids back home in Manhattan, and here you are suggesting that not only am I propositioning you but I'm betraying my…my darling husband's trust. Not to mention all the little rug-rats that my husband is caring for while I cart my sister halfway around the world.'

'Are you married?' he asked, startled at her not-so-coherent outburst, but she was already out of the car.

'That's none of your business,' she snapped. 'Oh, it might be if I was propositioning you, but, believe it or not, incredible as it might seem, I'm not propositioning you at all. So you can take your dinner invitation and shove it, Dr Cameron. We do not have a relationship. No relationship. Nix.'

'Kirsty…'

'What?' It was practically a snarl.

'Will you still do the hernia with me tomorrow morning?'

No apology, then. Did he really think she was making a pass at him? Of all the…

Swallow your anger, she told herself frantically. She was stuck here and she really wanted to do some medicine. She'd been bored for a month in Sydney. She didn't want to be bored here.

Swallow your pride.

'We can do your hernia if we stand at separate ends of the table and have an interpreter in the middle,' she muttered. 'After all, we can't talk if we don't have a relationship, and you're setting the rules. No relationship.'

'Kirsty, I'm sorry.' Finally an apology, she thought—but not a very good one.

'So am I,' she snapped. 'Because we might just have had a very nice dinner tonight. All of us. It might just have been what everyone needed. And we might just have had a decent working *relationship*. But it's not going to happen.'

She slammed the car door. Hard. She stomped into the castle forecourt. She could hear voices—laughter—coming from the kitchen gardens but she wasn't stopping to investigate.

She disappeared fast to her bedroom, she slammed the door and she didn't emerge until she heard Jake's car disappear down the road.

He'd gone. Taking his encumbrances with him.

Good.

Had he been stupid?

Jake worked for the rest of the day with a sense that he'd been an idiot. A huge idiot. A dinner invitation extended to all his family and hangers-on, and he'd reacted as Kirsty had said—as if she'd launched herself at him with the intention of ripping his clothes off.

So he had overreacted just a tad. Just a little.

But in a sense he knew he hadn't.

Evening surgery was boring. Coughs, colds, requests for repeat prescriptions, Mrs Bakerson's ever-troublesome knee, which responded only to fifteen minutes listening to how much trouble her kids were…there was nothing there to distract him from what he was thinking about.

He was thinking of Kirsty.

She was gorgeous.

She mightn't be thinking about relationships, he thought ruefully, but he definitely was. He just had to look at her—listen to her—watch the gentle way she interacted with Angus and with Mavis—and he wanted to take this further.

But she was married….

No, she wasn't married. She'd just thrown that into the ring to make him feel even more stupid about his repudiation of her dinner invitation.

It hadn't been a stupid repudiation.

She was a lovely, vibrant doctor with the world at her feet. She was building her career in Manhattan. She'd see her sister safely delivered and then the two of them would be off back to their life in the States.

Leaving him…

'Can you look at my big toe while I'm here?' Connie Bakerson was asking. 'The toenail's cutting in. You reckon I need an operation?'

He examined Connie's big toe with all seriousness. Diagnosis was easy. That was one of the good things about being a country doctor. He got the whole picture. Despite her troublesome knee, Connie and her husband spent every spare minute indulging their passion for line dancing. He'd noticed the appalling stiletto cowboy boots she wore, and he'd expected trouble ever since.

But he was still thinking about Kirsty. If he let himself fall in love...

How could he? There was no future in loving anyone except his twins. His girls were totally dependent on him, and he had little enough time for them now. If he spent the next few weeks falling in love with Kirsty and then she left...

Maybe he was being dumb, but he saw nothing down that road except heartache.

'You're not very chatty,' Connie commented, and he hauled himself to attention with an effort.

'I'm sorry.'

'You'll be thinking of those young ladies out at the castle,' Connie said with sudden perspicacity. 'Isn't it great that they're here? Everyone's talking about it. One of them pregnant with our Angus's great-nephew, and the other a doctor. What a combination.' She tugged her sock onto her foot and beamed. 'Wouldn't it be great if they stayed? Great for Angus. Great for you.'

'Why great for me?'

'Well, one of them being a doctor, of course,' Connie said, astonished. 'I hear she's already been out on a house-call with you and the locals are saying she's lovely.'

Of course, Jake thought bitterly. This was a tiny community. News travelled fast.

All the more reason not to think about Kirsty. If he so much as touched her, the news would be all over the district in minutes.

'Hey, maybe she's eligible,' Connie said, beaming some more. 'I hear she's really pretty. Both of them are lookers, they're saying, but the first poor lass has been battered. Knocked about in the car crash when her husband was killed, poor girl. But Harriet in the post office says the doctor one is a real stunner.' She raised her eyebrows in enquiry. 'So how about it, Doc? You've been single for far too long. Those poor wee mites need a mother.'

He was absolutely right in the way he'd reacted to Kirsty's invitation, Jake thought grimly as he managed a smile and showed Connie resolutely to the door. Kirsty thought he was inferring too much from one dinner invitation. She didn't know this town. They just had to see an eligible female and they started planning the wedding.

He just might nip this in the bud.

'I hear she's married,' he said, with something approaching malicious enjoyment. 'With six kids.'

'Six kids?' she said, astonished. 'No one told me that.'

'The village gossip network is letting you down. But she told me herself. She's taken time off to care for her sister but back home she has a poor, downtrodden husband changing diaper after diaper…'

'You're having me on.'

'She told me herself,' he said, virtuous and sure.

'Well!' Connie pulled herself up, figuring out whether to be indignant or not and deciding a little indignation was justified. 'Gallivanting over here when she has all those kiddies…'

'Awful, isn't it?'

'She must be real worried about her sister.'

'Maybe she's just tired of diapers.'

'We won't judge her,' Connie said resolutely. 'We need to know more. Your Margie was out there this morning, wasn't she?'

'She was.'

'I might just pop in to see Margie on the way home.'

'You do that,' Jake said, and suddenly he felt tired. 'See if you can find any more skeletons in the closet. Oh, and, Connie?'

'Mmm?'

'No dancing for a week.'

'But—'

'Some things I'm sure about,' Jake said. 'Not many, mind, but this is one of them. Sore knee. Sore big toe. I prescribe new boots and rest.'

'I can't rest.'

Not when there was gossip to be gleaned, Jake thought, watching through the window as she marched up the hill to visit Margie with nary a limp.

If ever he was going to have a relationship...how could he have it under the eyes of everyone in this town?

He wasn't having a relationship. End of story.

Move on to the next patient.

Kirsty woke the next morning to the sound of her sister whistling. Unable to believe her ears, she crossed to the window and looked outside.

The change in her two patients was extraordinary.

Susie was dressed and lying on a camping mattress they'd found yesterday. They'd cleaned it so Susie could lie on it while she gardened. The last of the rain had cleared. The day was already warm. Susie had a trowel in her hand, and she was digging around individual carrots.

Kirsty glanced up to Angus's window and Angus was perched in the window-seat, overseeing operations.

'You'll do yourself damage, girl,' he called. 'Wait until I get down to give you a hand.'

She was being put to shame by two invalids, Kirsty thought. Angus needed help dressing and he needed his oxygen checked and he was waiting for her.

Two people who thirty-six hours ago had wanted to die were now both aching for the day to begin.

Was she aching for her day to begin?

Maybe she was.

She was going to help Jake operate this morning, she remembered, but excitement wasn't exactly her overriding emotion.

Maybe there was also a tinge of fear.

Why fear? Was she fearful of the way she responded? Jake had let her know in no uncertain terms that he wanted nothing of that response.

She needed to ring Robert, she decided. Robert, her nice safe boyfriend back home. He was an optometrist she'd known for ever and their romance had been proceeding placidly—if tamely—when she'd had to leave with Susie.

She hadn't rung Robert for a week. It was time to get in touch with him again. Maybe he'd be surprised to hear from her. Their relationship was lacklustre at the best of times, and she suspected a month's absence was probably killing it for good, but she needed to ground herself somewhere and Robert was eternally useful.

Right. She'd ring Robert. After she'd telephoned Mavis Hipton to see how she'd got on in the night. After she'd organised Angus down to his garden. After she'd bullied Susie and Angus into eating breakfast.

But maybe the bullying wouldn't be because they weren't interested in eating, she thought suddenly. It would be bullying because they'd be too busy to eat.

Suddenly Susie and Angus were excited by life again.

She needed to get excited, too.

She was going to operate with Jake.

She was excited.

There was no relationship, she told herself crossly.

No—but she was still excited.

CHAPTER FIVE

DOLPHIN BAY Bush Nursing Hospital was a neat little building made of the deep grey stone of the local cliffs. It had wide verandas and a lovely, rambling garden, and as she pulled into the parking lot she could see half a dozen people pottering in the flower-beds. There were glimpses of the sea through the tangle of honeysuckle and bougainvillea, and a flock of white galahs was screeching and fighting for places on the branches of the towering gums.

She should transplant this place to Manhattan, she thought longingly. What a wonderful place to die.

What a wonderful place to live.

They all knew who she was. The moment she climbed out of the car she was watched, by the gardeners and by the patients sitting in the sun on the veranda, and a chirpy young nurse bustled out to greet her.

'You'll be Dr Kirsty. I'm Babs. We've been waiting for you.'

Dr Kirsty. Babs. This was as formal as it got in Dolphin Bay, Kirsty thought wryly, but she grinned.

'Dr Cam— Dr Jake said to be here at ten.'

'Yes, but Francis is in such a state that if we don't knock him out soon, he'll do a runner,' Babs told her. She ushered her inside and flung open the theatre doors. 'It's OK, Jake. Kirsty's here.'

Jake was already in theatre gear. He was systematically checking equipment but as Kirsty walked in he turned and smiled, and her heart did that crazy backflip she was starting to recognise. And starting to resent. Darn, why didn't she get that backflip when Robert smiled?

This man didn't want a relationship. Not!

'You've been waiting for me?' she managed.

'We have the world's scaredest patient,' he told her. 'Francis is sixty years old. Until his hernia got bad he was our local fire chief. Put him in front of wildfire and he'll be the coolest head in the district, but show him a drop of blood and he'll faint. He's still in his room. I thought if we wheeled him along here and he caught sight of theatre gear, he might end up dying of shock.'

'I'll check him there, then, shall I?' she asked, and he smiled again.

'If you would. Is there anything else here that you need?'

She did a fast check. This should be a simple procedure—a simple anaesthetic. Even catering for terror.

The little theatre looked brilliant.

'How many beds does the hospital have?' she asked in surprise.

'Twenty. Plus ten nursing-home beds.'

'That's too many for one doctor.'

'You're telling me. I have to work hard to keep them healthy.'

'Jake makes his patients work in the garden,' Babs said cheekily from the doorway. 'He has a method of bowel control that's second to none. You stay regular or you get garden duty.'

'You're kidding.'

'He gives out garden duty for everything,' Babs continued. 'You just sigh in this place and someone sticks a trowel in your hand.'

'Don't the patients object?'

'They love it,' Jake said, attempting a glower at the nurse. 'Babs, go introduce Kirsty to Francis. I want him back here asleep in ten minutes.'

'That's if my checks are OK,' Kirsty said, attempting to find some vestige of authority.

'They will be,' Babs said. 'Otherwise you'll be handed a trowel as well. Our Dr Jake runs a tight ship.'

* * *

There was no need for the trowel.

Francis was a big man, but he'd kept himself fit, he didn't smoke and he had no underlying medical conditions to give her concern. The only problem was his terror, which was palpable the moment she entered the room.

'Hi. I'm Dr Kirsty, your anaesthetist. I'm here to make you relax enough for Jake to fix your bump.' Then she hesitated. The man was physically cringing. 'Am I so scary?'

'N-no, but…'

'Does your wife ever get her hair set at the hairdresser? Does she ever sit under a dryer?'

'Sure,' he whispered, not knowing where this was going.

'Well, I don't want to scare you any more than you already are, but your wife has more chance of getting electrocuted under the dryer than you do of getting damaged by my anaesthetic. But Dr Jake's telling me you're scared.'

'I'm not…it's not…'

'It's not logical,' she said, smiling and lifting his wrist, ostensibly to feel his pulse but in reality to give him the comfort of touch. 'I know. Like I'm scared of moths. I can't stand them; they make my hair stand on end. But if I had to face them in order to fix my life…'

'You would?'

'Actually, I wouldn't,' she conceded with a rueful smile. 'Not without a lot of screaming and running and general loss of dignity. What I might do, though—if I had to face them—is ask a nice doctor to give me something to make me sleepy and dreamy and away with the fairies, so that any moth could go bump into me and I'd simply wave and smile.'

That drew a reluctant smile. 'You're saying you could give me something like that.'

'Ooh, the very nicest of drugs,' she told him. 'Guaranteed to make you smile and wave till the cows come home.'

'Till the cows come home,' he said, dazed. 'I thought you were from New York?'

'I'm learning the local lingo,' she said, with a certain amount of pride. 'Australian country talk. I can talk about mates and blokes and anything to do with a heap of dung you care to mention. I think I have an ear for languages. Now I'm staying with Angus, it's Australian with a Scottish accent. So will you let me give you my hallucinogenic substance?'

He seemed even more dazed. Terror had receded in the face of her ridiculousness. 'It'll make me go to sleep?' he managed, but he didn't sound as if it was a dreadful idea.

'No,' she told him. 'Not my dream stuff. It'll simply make you relax. Then, if it's OK with you—and only if it's OK with you—we can take the next step and give you something so you have a swift sleep while Dr Jake fixes your bump. If you don't feel relaxed then you can back out. But you do want your hernia fixed, right?'

'Right,' he whispered.

'You really do?'

'Y-yes.'

'Well done,' she told him, releasing his wrist and touching the back of his weathered hand lightly with her own. 'There's courage and there's courage. My moths and your anaesthetic. You want to start now?'

'Y— Maybe.'

'Then let's do step one,' she told him. 'You close your eyes while Babs holds your hand, you'll feel one tiny prick, then we'll see if my fairy dust works. We can take it from there.'

She administered the propofol, then stood and chatted some more, watching as his eyes became confused—but not terrified at all. She was even making him smile.

'Next step?' she asked, and got a sleepy, fuzzy nod for her pains.

Hooray. She needed to let Jake know they were due to start.

She heard a faint movement in the doorway and turned, expecting to see an orderly.

But it was Jake.

He was looking at her with blatant admiration.

How long had he been here? She felt a blush starting at her toes and working its way up. This man had the power to seriously unsettle her. He was almost as unsettling as moths,

'You're good,' he told her, and she struggled for composure—struggled to give him her very smuggest smile.

'I know,' she told him. 'Francis and I are developing a very nice relationship. Aren't you sorry you're not into relationships yourself?'

She shouldn't have said it.

The operation was done in almost total silence. The atmosphere was so tense it was almost unbearable. Not only did he not want to take their relationship any further, she'd killed any friendship they might have been starting to build.

Which was a shame.

She very much wanted to keep working with him, she decided as she watched his fingers perform the delicate piece of surgery to relieve Francis of his hernia. It wasn't a particularly difficult operation, but his fingers were swift and sure. He was meticulous in everything he did. Francis would be left with minimal scarring and a super-fast recovery because of it.

He was a seriously good surgeon, she thought. He was wasted in Dolphin Bay.

And then she thought, no, he wasn't wasted in Dolphin Bay. A place like this was lucky to have him. Susie would be blessed to have him if she got into trouble at delivery. If every country town could have a doctor as good as Jake…

'Blood pressure?' Jake snapped, and she told him, aware that she'd been watching him for a moment and this was a ruse to make her look at her dials instead of looking at him. She flushed. There was no need to remind her to do her job. He might be a good surgeon, but she knew enough about anaesthesia for her attention never to stray away for more than a second or two at a time. Francis's anaesthetic was the lightest she could give. She had him intubated but his vital signs were steady, his colour was great and every indication was that this surgery would cause him minimal discomfort.

'Reverse,' Jake snapped.

She raised an eyebrow. 'Say please,' she said mildly, and Babs choked.

Jake glared. 'What?'

'Say please…sir.'

'Kirsty…'

'Politeness is everything. We may as well start the way we mean to go on.'

'Please,' he said, goaded, and she smiled.

'That's better,' she approved. She turned to Babs. 'He's very autocratic for a surgeon, isn't he? I thought you had to be at least an orthodontist before you let go of the *please*.'

'Can we concentrate on what's important?' Jake snapped, and she very nearly said *Say please* again.

Then she glanced at his face and saw the lines of strain around his eyes and thought better of it.

Whatever was eating him, she wasn't going to break through with laughter.

She probably wasn't going to break through at all.

'Is it over?' Francis surfaced terrified, his eyes wild and frantic. Jake was hauling his gloves off and Kirsty leaned over, took Francis's hands in hers and held. Hard.

'It's done. You've conquered your fear. You're awake. Jake's fixed your hernia, your wife is waiting to see you and all you have to show is a three-inch square dressing on your tummy. Six stitches. When you wake up a bit more, you can have a look.'

'It's done?'

'It is. The operation is completely finished. All that's left is my fairy dust, making you a bit sleepy. If I were you, I'd settle back for a nice long nap.'

He searched her eyes, hope warring with fear, dreading that she might not be telling the truth.

But then Jake was behind her, gripping her shoulder, presenting them as a team.

'She's right, mate. You're a new man. Thanks to our Dr Kirsty.'

'She's a ripper,' Francis whispered. 'A real ripper.'

'Not a particularly respectful ripper,' Jake said steadily. 'But a ripper for all that.'

Francis closed his eyes. Jake stepped back, releasing Kirsty. The orderly moved in to wheel the trolley back out into the corridor. Jake moved into the washroom, but Kirsty stood still for a while longer.

Until the sensation of fingers pressing against her shoulder was completely gone.

He had a list.

The hernia had been a test, she realised. By the time she'd got rid of her hospital gown Jake was waiting for her, and he handed her a slip of paper.

   Dorothy Miller: Veins
   Mark Glaston: Basal cell carcinoma
   Scotty Anderson: Osteochondroma

'What's this?' she asked cautiously. She was in the corridor outside Theatre. Maybe they could have gone somewhere else to talk. Jake must have an office, she thought, but maybe showing her into an office might get her alone. That might constitute a relationship.

'Look, I'm sorry,' he said, sounding exasperated, and she knew she didn't have to say it out loud for him to know what she was thinking. 'I overreacted yesterday.'

'You did.'

'So don't rub it in.'

'Tell me about the list,' she said coolly, and there was a

moment's hesitation while he considered whether to take her antagonism further. But he obviously—and wisely—decided against it.

'Dorothy Miller has the most appalling varicose veins,' he told her. 'One burst last month and it came close to killing her. She's eighty and she won't go to the city to get them fixed. She says if she dies she dies, but I'd prefer her not to. Mark has a basal cell carcinoma on his face that's been incompletely excised. He needs a full-thickness excision and a skin graft. It's a simple job, but Mark's wife is blind, they have two small children and for him to leave for a night is a major drama. I told him he'd have to find a way and he agreed, but now you're here I'll do it myself.'

'Now that I've proved myself competent,' she said dryly, and he had the grace to smile.

'As you say.'

'And the osteochondroma?'

Bony growths where they shouldn't be were a common childhood problem so it was no surprise when he said, 'Scotty is four years old. The osteochondroma is on his leg. I biopsied it and it's fine but it's growing. Scotty's mother is a single mum with three other littlies dependent on her. It'd be a heck of a lot easier if we did it here.'

'So you really do need me,' she said, cheering up, and he looked a bit shamefaced.

'Um…yes.' There was another momentary hesitation. 'What you did with Mavis… I've been out there this morning and she tells me you've already phoned and adjusted the dose. But already the change is miraculous. And here…all these things can wait, but as you're here and not busy…'

'You may as well use me,' she agreed. She paused, and then decided to push it. 'You know, you really do need to learn to chat to me, though,' she told him. 'I'm not accustomed to silence. Maybe we can get piped music in Theatre. Or piped gossip. That's what I'm used to back home.'

His face stayed expressionless. 'Silence makes for concentration.'

'Sure, and you need to concentrate really hard on a hernia op. It's nail-biting life-and-death drama.'

'You're being silly.'

'You don't think it's you who's being silly?'

'Am I?' he demanded. 'Kirsty, leave it.'

But the look on his face was making her angry all over again. It was like he was afraid of her. As if he was wary that she'd push him into something he didn't want.

'I don't want this,' he added, and she glowered.

'Don't.'

'Don't what?'

'Don't you push this any further,' she warned. 'If you're about to say something about me feeling what you're feeling and it's not wise, or that you're instinctively realising that I want your body but you don't want me, or really you'd love to make mad, passionate love to me but you're a closet gay…'

There was the sound of choking and Babs was goggle-eyed behind them. The nurse had her hand to her mouth, as if she'd tried to keep herself silent but failed. Just as well, Kirsty thought. She was way out of line.

She collected herself. Sort of. Just for a moment there she'd almost been enjoying herself, hauling the self-contained Dr Jake Cameron right out of his comfort zone.

'Don't mind me,' she managed, turning and smiling at Babs. 'I'm an American. We're known for being forward, if not downright ridiculous.' She turned back to Jake. 'But, of course, I'll do your list, Dr Cameron. Any time. Anywhere. But not now, as I'm off home to our castle to check on Angus and Susie.' She took another deep breath and almost recovered.

'Don't fret that you were eavesdropping,' she said finally to Babs. 'What you heard—very clearly—was me *not* propositioning your Dr Jake.'

* * *

What was it with the man? All the way home she fumed, trying to figure out what her hormones were doing to her. Why was she feeling like this?

Jake wasn't the only one who didn't do relationships. Kirsty had no intention of letting herself go down that route.

She'd learned early. When Kirsty and Susie had been ten their mother had died unexpectedly and tragically of a sub-arachnoid haemorrhage. They'd all been devastated—of course—but their father had been passionately in love with his wife and he'd never recovered.

Two years after his wife had died, Taylor McMahon had taken his own life, leaving his little girls to a succession of foster-homes.

Love must be appalling to do that to you, Kirsty had reasoned, and she'd decided then and there that she'd never let herself feel that way about anyone but Susie.

When Susie had met Rory…for a little while Kirsty had let herself start believing again in happy-ever-after. Only then Rory had died. Of course. The whole appalling cycle had started again—trying to drag someone you loved back from the brink.

It wasn't going to happen to her. She dated nice safe men who left her emotionally free. That was the way of survival. Nice safe Robert…

If Jake thought she'd threaten that by falling for him, he had to be joking.

So cut it out, she told herself. Quit it with the hormones. The man is seriously threatening to your peace of mind. As well as that, he's seriously committed to his twins and you're not the least bit interested in playing Mom. Even if he was interested. Even if you're interested. Which you're not.

A ready-made family would be the pits.

She pulled into the castle forecourt and Jake's two little girls came racing out the front door to meet her. There goes that argument, she thought bitterly as they tugged open her car door. These two buttons were seriously cute.

'We saw you coming from upstairs,' Alice announced—or was it Penelope? They were identically dressed in miniature jeans and grubby windcheaters. Their shoes were caked with mud, and their curls were escaping from the crimson ribbons at the ends of their pigtails. 'Angus went for a nap and Susie said we had to go up and tell him that Spike's measurement is a whole half-inch wider than yesterday. Mr Boyce says Spike's going to be ginormous.'

'And Boris got paw marks all over Angus's bed when we let him in,' her twin announced, big with importance in the telling of such a tale. 'Margie growled, and then she saw our muddy shoes. She told us we were rascals and we had to hop it—but Angus says he likes rascals. Then we saw your car so we thought we might hop it anyway.'

'So we hopped all the way down the stairs,' the other twin explained again, grinning a hugely appealing gap-toothed grin. 'The stairs here are beeyootiful. Penelope can hop three stairs at a time and I nearly can but not all the time.'

'You need practice,' Kirsty said, smiling as she climbed out of the car. She looked behind the twins to where Susie was balancing on crutches in the doorway. Her twin was smiling, and Kirsty had a sudden vision of how her own twin had looked when she had been this age. They must have both looked like this, she thought. Happy, bubbly little girls with not a care between them.

Susie's smile was like that now, she thought in surprise. It was an echo of the past when as twins they'd done their own hopping. Before life had got in the way and they'd realised the damage love could cause. But Susie's smile had been resurrected by this place. By Angus and by Jake and by these two little girls.

Don't you dare let your hormones mess with this, she told herself fiercely. Start acting professionally with Dr Cameron.

'Margie says as soon as you come back, we have to go home,' one of the twins was saying. They grabbed a hand each and started tugging her toward the door. 'But you have to see Spike first. We want to show you ourselves. He's humungous and Susie said he's getting humungouser.'

'Humungouser?' she said faintly, and from the doorway Susie giggled. It was a great sound, Kirsty thought. It had been so long since Susie had giggled regularly.

'He's a wonderful pumpkin,' she managed, trying not to sound choked up.

'Please, can we stay for lunch?' a twin was begging. 'We'll ring Daddy and tell him we have to. Mr Boyce is out minding Spike, and Margie says he's as happy as a pig in mud and we can stay for lunch as long as you say it's OK and so does Daddy.'

'What do you think?' Kirsty asked her twin, when she could get a word in edgeways, and Susie's smile broadened.

'I think these kids are great.'

'I think this place is great,' Kirsty told her.

'Did you have fun with Jake this morning?'

Kirsty eyed her twin with caution. The problem with being a twin was that you were known too well.

'We did a very satisfactory operation.'

'That's nice,' Susie said demurely.

Kirsty thought, Yep, she'd been sussed.

'But can we stay?' the twins said plaintively.

'You ring Jake and ask if the girls can stay for lunch,' she told Susie.

'You don't want to?'

'Dr Cameron and I have what's becoming a very cool relationship,' she retorted. 'So don't get any ideas.'

'Me?' Susie asked, starting forward on her crutches with an ease that Kirsty found extraordinary. 'When have I ever? Oh, by the way, Robert called. He said to say he was sorry he missed you this morning. He's going out of town for the weekend but he might find time to ring you on Monday. Now, *that*,' she told the little girls as they tugged Kirsty forward to join her sister, 'that's what a really passionate relationship ought to be.'

'Susie…' Kirsty said warningly, and that delicious chuckle sounded out again.

'I know. I'm sticking my nose in where it's not wanted. But I'm enjoying myself and, oh, Kirsty, it feels so good.'

The twins and the Boyces were permitted to stay.

'Jake sounded really reluctant,' Susie reported after phoning. 'He kept saying he didn't want the twins to be any trouble, but how can they be when Margie and Ben are here? Margie is lovely and she says she'd much rather babysit here than back in the village.'

It was hard to figure out who was babysitting who, Kirsty thought as the afternoon wore on. After lunch, by common consensus, they returned to the vegetable patch to superintend Spike's growth spurt. Angus and Ben perched on a garden bench in the sun and discussed the merits of different varieties of pumpkin. Susie lay on her mattress, alternatively dozing and supervising Alice and Penelope making mud pies. Margie sat herself down on a rocker on the porch, knitting and listening to her favourite radio show. We look like the Brady Bunch, Kirsty thought suddenly. All contentment and calm.

Who knew what was seething underneath?

She grinned at herself, and her twin saw the grin and demanded an explanation.

'Domesticity plus,' she said, and Susie gave a sleepy smile.

'Jake should be here. It's sad that he spends so little time with his girls. You should help him more while you're here, Kirsty, so he can be free.'

'I'm doing my best,' she said stiffly.

The doorbell rang. Or, as Kirsty had now learned, the bell on the intercom connected to the gate rang.

'We're not home,' Susie said with a yawn. 'This is perfect. We don't need anyone else.'

They didn't. But it might be Jake. He did have a right to be here. And maybe…maybe he could stay for a while, Kirsty thought. Then she gave herself a harsh mental slap for the thought. But she did get up to go and open the gate.

Professional relationship, she told herself firmly as she walked out to the castle entrance.

But before she got there she realised she'd made a mistake, It wouldn't be Jake. He had a key and his own remote controller for the gates.

But she was already at the entrance. She might as well see who…

It wasn't an insurance salesman. She opened the door and it was a man who looked like Rory.

'Rory,' she said—blankly—unable to believe her eyes. But, of course, she had to be mistaken. Susie's husband had been dead for six months. And when she looked closer this man was different. He had a slighter build, different hair colour, different features…

Different but the same.

'I'm Kenneth Douglas,' he told her, and all was explained. Rory's brother was Kenneth. Kirsty had never seen him. Susie had met him once, just before Rory had been killed, and she'd reported that he was a creep.

But he was here. He was Rory's brother.

'Hi,' she said, holding out her hand in greeting. 'I'm Susie's sister, Kirsty.'

'Susie?' he said blankly.

'Rory's wife, Susie.'

His face froze. 'Rory's wife is here?'

'Yes.'

'She has no right.'

'Angus seems to think she's very welcome,' Kirsty told him, struggling to keep her smile in place. She hesitated, not wanting this man to interrupt their lovely afternoon but knowing that he was Angus's nephew, knowing that he was Rory's brother. She had no grounds for denying him entrance. 'We're all in the vegetable garden,' she told him. 'Do you want me to take you through?'

'Who's in the vegetable garden?'

'Your uncle—'

'Angus isn't here.' It was an appalled hiss. 'He's in a nursing home. He was moving there yesterday. He's dying.'

Grief and fear did odd things to people, Kirsty knew. She wasn't tempted to react to this with anger.

'I don't think he is dying,' she said gently. 'We've persuaded him that oxygen will help, and it's been wonderful. He's back gardening.'

'The doctor said he was going into a nursing home.'

'Now we're here, he doesn't have to leave. He can stay for as long as he wants.'

'We?' the man said, and there was no doubting that his over-riding emotion was anger. 'Who's we?'

'My sister and I.'

'Your sister has no right,' he hissed again. 'Who the hell does she think she is? I thought she was too badly injured to travel. I thought she was done with.'

She wanted to slam the door in his face at that, but it was too late. He was through.

'Look, Mr Douglas—'

'I want to see her,' he said, and he was striding toward the vegetable garden so fast she practically had to run to keep up. 'If she's messing with the old man's treatment—if she thinks there's anything here for her... Rory's dead and I'm the only one who has any say in how the old man is treated. Me.'

'I'm sorry, but...' He'd reached the side gate and he hauled it open while she struggled to think how to deflect him. There was no way. He'd hauled open the gate and was staring through at the scene of domesticity in front of him.

Angus and Ben discussing pumpkins.

Alice and Penelope turning their skills from mud pies to mud sausages—arguing over whose was the longest.

Margie knitting.

And Susie, rising on one elbow to see who it was. Susie, recognising Kenneth's face and trying, falteringly, to smile a welcome. Susie pushing herself into a sitting position. Hampered by her weakness and her advanced pregnancy.

'Kenneth,' she whispered.

Kirsty glanced again at Rory's brother and got a shock.

Every vestige of colour had drained from his face. If she hadn't reached forward fast and supported him, he would have fallen. He slumped, and she had to assist him to sit on the low stone wall by the gate.

He put his head in his hands and she could see him visibly brace. Stiffen. Look up.

'You're pregnant,' he said in a voice of loathing, of fury and of pure shock. 'You're pregnant with Rory's child.'

CHAPTER SIX

For a moment no one spoke. The twins stared open-mouthed. Mrs Boyce's knitting needles stilled and Angus sat back on his heels and gazed at his nephew like he was seeing a ghost.

'Kenneth.' There was lingering affection in his voice, Kirsty thought. Once he'd loved this man. As a boy?

'You're supposed to be dead,' Kenneth snarled and any hint of affection, any trace of warmth in the sun-filled afternoon was gone.

'I'm not,' Angus said warily, putting a hand on his oxygen cylinder as if assuring himself it was still available.

'I rang that bloody doctor last week and he said you were going into a home yesterday and you were dying.'

'I said if no one cared enough to come, then he'd die.'

Kirsty hadn't noticed Jake's arrival but he was suddenly right behind him. He must have driven though the gates after Kenneth's arrival, and she had been so caught up that she hadn't heard. Now Kenneth rose, his colour flooding back. 'You,' he said, and his fury seemed to be escalating by the moment, redirecting itself to Jake. 'You lied.'

'Kenneth, take care,' Jake said warningly. 'There's no need for you to think people here are against you. Would you like to meet my twins?'

He was trying to defuse the situation, Kirsty realised. She looked at the fury on Kenneth's face and thought this had to be some sort of mental illness. Surely such anger couldn't be justified?

But Kenneth was whirling again to stare at Susie. 'She's pregnant,' he whispered. 'Pregnant.'

'Susie's pregnant with Rory's baby, yes,' Jake said evenly. 'We all think that's great.'

'And she'll inherit…' He choked, and Kirsty realised he'd gone past logic. 'She'll inherit from Rory…'

'Rory's dead, Ken,' Jake said evenly. 'Susie won't inherit anything from anyone.'

'The b—'

'Get out of my garden.' It was Angus. He was as pale as the night they'd arrived but he had himself under control. He held on to his oxygen cylinder as if he needed its support, but when he spoke his voice was completely steady. 'If you insult Rory's wife, you're not welcome in my home.'

'It's not your home. You should be dead.'

'Jake,' Angus said tiredly, and Jake gave an almost imperceptible nod.

'Ken, let's go,' he said softly. He took Kenneth's arm and when Ken tried—violently—to wrench away, his hold tightened. 'You're not welcome here, mate,' he said softly. 'You know you can't speak to people like this and stay welcome.' He propelled him around, facing away from the others in the garden. 'Come with me,' he said softly. 'Something tells me you've been skipping medication. I can help you if you'll come with me. Come back and talk to your uncle when you're feeling calmer.'

'Don't touch me.' He wrenched with even more fury and because he was hauling backward, toward the gate, Jake let him go. Then suddenly he smashed forward again. But Jake must have been expecting it. As Ken blundered past he caught his arm, twisted, held. He had him locked against him, his arms up behind his back.

'Ken, we're going to the hospital, mate,' he said softly.

'I don't need—'

'You need help.' Despite the violence, shocking in such a peaceful setting, Jake was speaking as if nothing untoward had happened. 'You know you're supposed to be on medication. You told me last time, carbamazepine.'

'She's pregnant. It's *mine*.'

'Kirsty, could you help me take Ken to the hospital?' Jake asked. He smiled across at his little girls, standing open-mouthed and frightened. 'Guys, Mr Douglas is ill. His head's hurting and it's making him say things he doesn't mean. Dr Kirsty and I will take him away and make him feel better. Margie and Mr Boyce and Susie and Angus will stay and look after you. Is that OK?'

They stared a bit more but they almost visibly relaxed in the face of their father's normal tone.

'OK,' Penelope whispered—or was it Alice?

'That's great.' Ken seemed to have slumped against Jake, suddenly passive. He glanced across at Kirsty. 'You want to drive or sit in the back with our passenger?'

'I think I'll drive,' she said faintly. 'If it's OK with you.'

The drive back to the hospital was made in grim silence. Ken didn't appear to object, which made Kirsty wonder how often these sort of outbursts had happened in the past. He seemed almost resigned.

At the hospital Jake administered a small dose of chlorpromazine and organised a hospital bed, and then he sat with Ken as he drifted into sleep. Kirsty could have disappeared then, but she didn't. She needed to know about this man's anger, she decided. The way he'd reacted to Susie had been terrifying.

So she made herself a coffee at the nurses' station and waited for Jake to reappear. He finally emerged, looking grim. When he saw her, he seemed to make an effort to make his face relax.

'I thought you'd have gone home.'

'I'm driving your car,' she reminded him. 'That would have left you stuck.'

'There are hospital cars, or one of the locals would have driven me back.'

'I wanted to know about Ken. He hates Susie. Why?'

'Ken hates the world,' Jake said bluntly. He started making himself a coffee, talking to her as if he was thinking aloud. 'Ken was born with a personality disorder that makes him think the world's against him. Angus tells me that having him here as a child was a nightmare—he was so jealous of Rory that he made life unbearable. Angus saw little of him over the last few years, but lately he's been badgering me about Angus's health. I figure he thinks Angus is going to die soon and he'll inherit. Today's behaviour confirmed that. But his behaviour is way out of normal bounds. He's seriously ill.'

'What can you do about it?'

'I'm not sure,' he told her. 'His behaviour today was so bizarre that in the old days I'd have had him committed.'

'Not so easy today, huh?'

'I'd imagine it'd be just the same in the States as it is here,' he told her. 'Evidence of gross psychiatric disturbance and the sworn statements of two psychiatrists that he forms a risk. What I should have done was let him slug someone today. Then I could have got him arrested. But the nearest person was me and I'm not all that into being slugged for the greater good.'

'I don't blame you.' She hesitated. 'What now?'

'I can hold him here overnight,' he told her. 'I've probably gone further than wise in giving him a dose of chlorpromazine that'll knock him out. He could probably sue as he didn't agree to it. But I'm hoping that a solid sleep will leave him calmer. I'll make an urgent call to the state psychiatric database people and see if I can find someone who knows him. Then I'll try and get him on some sort of calming medication. But he doesn't have to agree to it, and maybe once he's had a sleep and is back to being logical he won't want it.'

'Is he functioning?'

'You mean does he make a habit of verging on violence for

no reason? No. Angus has talked about him to me. He's suffered from uncontrollable rage from childhood but he's somehow kept it under limits enough for him to function. He's a qualified accountant, working in Sydney. He's had two brief failed marriages, so he must seem normal most of the time.'

'But not today,' she said—and shivered.

'No.' Jake looked at her like he was looking straight through her, seeing the problems on the other side. 'Maybe he saw the ramifications of Susie's baby more clearly than either Angus or Susie have seen it yet. They're so delighted to find each other that they haven't seen what's obvious.'

'Which is?'

'Angus is an exceedingly wealthy man,' Jake said gently. 'Although he downplays it, he has a title many people would give their eye teeth for. He also has entailed property back in Scotland. Loganaich is a major seat and Angus has a rent roll that would make your head spin. Angus told me once that he'd never wanted it, but it's entailed in such a way he couldn't avoid inheriting. He said Rory felt the same. Angus was devastated when Rory died, because the next in line—'

'Is Kenneth,' she breathed. 'Oh, no.'

'Maybe not Kenneth any more,' he said sombrely. 'Maybe Susie's baby.'

Kirsty's breath sucked in as the repercussions sank home. 'So today…'

'For the last few months—since Rory's death—Kenneth must have believed that he'll be the next Earl of Loganaich, with all the wealth and privilege that entails. Today he saw Susie's pregnancy and he realised his calculations were wrong. I watched his face. He looked angry when he saw that Angus was using oxygen—that there'll be a delay before he inherits. But when he realised Susie was pregnant, he almost passed out.'

'She won't want wealth,' Kirsty whispered. 'She'd never want it.'

'I figured that,' Jake said gently. 'Finally. You just have to know you, Kirsty, to know what a loving, giving person Susie must be.'

'Don't,' she said distressfully. 'You know nothing about us. Rory and Ken were brothers and they're so different.'

'Kenneth's ill. You're not ill,' he said softly. 'Kirsty…'

'Leave it, Jake,' she said harshly. The hospital corridor was deserted and she felt suddenly exposed. How could he say such things to her and not mean…? Not mean anything?

She didn't want him to mean anything.

'So what do we do about Kenneth?' she asked, louder than she'd intended, and she flushed. 'I mean…'

'There's not a lot we can do,' he said, his eyes still thoughtful. But he wasn't thinking about Kenneth, she thought suddenly, and her flush deepened. 'As I said, I'll try and find a psychiatrist who knows him and get some advice. I'll try and arrange transport to one of the better psychiatric institutions. We can only hope that when he wakes up he's come to terms with the new order.'

'He never thought he'd inherit before,' she said, struggling to move past her emotions. 'Not until Rory died.'

'So we hold to that. Maybe it'll be fine.'

'How can it be anything but fine?'

'That's right,' he said, but he looked worried as he glanced at his watch. 'I might get the Boyces and the kids to stay on at the castle for the rest of the day,' he went on slowly. 'It'll take everyone's mind off what's happened and…'

'And it'll provide more security for Angus and Susie?'

'It will,' he said gravely, and then he paused for a moment and kept on thinking. 'You know, the castle is very big. There's lots of bedrooms.'

'You're thinking of filling them?'

'It might be fun for the Boyces and the twins,' he told her. 'Not to mention Susie and Angus. I'll phone Angus and run it past him. Maybe I'll say it'll make you free to help me.'

'If the twins stay there…'

'I'll stay there, too,' he said. 'Just until I know Kenneth's out of the district.' He hesitated and then confessed, 'He makes me nervous.'

'Me, too.'

'And we should be able to keep our hands off each other for a few days.'

She stiffened. What on earth was he playing at?

'I don't know about your hands but my hands haven't got the slightest inclination to wander your way,' she snapped. 'Unless it's to give you a good swipe across the ears. Of all the arrogant, egotistical statements...'

'You do feel it, too.'

'Get lost,' she retorted, the emotions of the afternoon venting themselves in anger. 'Take your rotten feelings and play with them somewhere else. I have no idea what you're talking about.' And she turned and stalked out of the hospital with her nose in the air.

'How will you get home?' he called after her.

'I'll walk.'

'Wait a few minutes and I'll drive you.'

'I wouldn't trust myself,' she managed without pausing. 'You and me in a car with all that molten passion... We'd be a road safety risk, Jake Cameron. I'm not coming near you again until you have your passion safely in a glass jar in a locked cabinet. And me... I'm taking my molten whatever for a good long walk.'

She stalked out—past the unsuspecting Babs, who was just coming in.

'Molten passion?' Babs asked. 'Am I missing something?'

'We both are,' Kirsty told her with a tired smile. 'Dr Cameron and I have just admitted a patient with psychiatric disturbances, but if I were you I'd be worrying about who's treating who. As far as psychiatric disturbances go, it might be a case of physician heal thyself.'

And she left, with Babs staring after her.

She didn't know whether Jake was staring after her. She didn't trust herself to look back and find out.

* * *

It was a long walk but she needed it. By the time she reached home she was only just nearing a state where she could think with anything approaching calm. And that was only when she very carefully made herself think of anything other than Jake Cameron.

She walked into the forecourt and swung the gate closed behind her. Home, she thought, and then gave a wry grin. Two days ago could she ever have imagined herself thinking of this crazy place as home? But she made her way to the bathroom and greeted Queen Victoria almost like a friend.

It'd be OK. Kenneth might be threatening but this place was built like a fortress after all.

'You and me will keep them safe,' she told Queen V. 'We don't need any Jake Cameron.'

She got a disapproving look for her pains. Victoria had had her Albert, and then her Mr Brown. Was she egging Kirsty on toward the involvement she'd always forsworn?

'I don't need anyone,' Kirsty declared, more than a little self-consciously, and went to find the rest of the castle inhabitants. She might not *need* anyone but a little company would be nice. If only to stop her talking to dead monarchs!

In the end it was harder to find someone to talk to than she'd thought. Angus and Susie and the twins were all asleep. Finally she tracked down Margie who was peeling potatoes in the kitchen while Ben supervised.

'It seems you're stuck with us, dear,' Margie said, welcoming her with a wave of a floury hand as Kirsty entered. 'I hope you don't mind, but I thought I'd make pasties for dinner.'

'Jake's talked to you?'

'Dr Jake's talked to His Lordship and he's talked to us. We all think it's a fine idea. Don't we, Ben?'

Ben, a wisp of a man who'd practically disappeared in the fireside chair, nodded emphatically.

'Kenneth is a worry to us all,' he said gravely. 'Angus is very upset. It took his mind right off his pumpkin.'

'But we've reassured him,' Margie assured her. 'He and

Susie were in a right state, but the twins decided mud pies were boring so we've made brambleberry pies instead. There's a great patch right outside the gate. I had everyone pick while I made the pastry and it's kept everyone nicely distracted. Now we've all eaten so much it's coming out our ears—there's some in the pantry for you, lass.'

This was real medicine. Kirsty served herself pie—still warm—and decided maybe Kenneth needed pie instead of tranquillisers. If only it were that easy.

But for Susie and Angus it had been that easy. They'd been distressed and they'd been cured by a big dose of family.

Jake's idea of everyone staying together was an excellent plan, she decided, and she wondered again about the difficulties of being a country doctor.

Jake had been upset that she knew more about palliative medicine than he did, but his cures were so much more diverse. He'd looked at this problem and he'd cured it by a case of lateral thinking. But...

'How can you all just move into the castle?' Kirsty asked, confused, and Margie raised her eyebrows in astonishment.

'Wouldn't you come here if you were asked? There's not a person in this district who wouldn't give their right arm for such an invitation. My Ben here and His Lordship go back a long way. They've been comparing pumpkins for ever. And with Ben's arthritis we don't get out all that much any more. When Jake rang and suggested it we thought, well, it sounds just like a holiday. Now you're here, I'll pop back home and get our night things...'

'And water our veggie garden,' Ben said from his cavernous chair.

'It rained yesterday so there's no need,' his wife said serenely. 'You see, no trouble.'

'But... Jake...' Kirsty said slowly. This was so far away from the city medical practice she knew that it seemed a different world. Jake was worried about his patients so he moved in with them? Unbelievable.

'I think our Kenneth has put the wind right up our doctor,' Margie said, watching her face and guessing her thoughts. 'Mind, it'll be good for him to be out here for a bit as well. His hospital apartment's a dreary place.'

'Why doesn't he find himself somewhere nicer to live?'

'Practicalities, dear,' Margie told her. 'When he first came he bought himself a lovely home a few blocks from the hospital but, of course, he's the only doctor and if he's called during the night then there's no one to take care of the girls. Ben and I come in during the day but he's an independent man. He doesn't want a live-in nanny.'

'So what does he do now?'

'His apartment is a part of the hospital. When he gets called out at night, the nursing staff take over caring for the twins. Minimum disruption. But being by the hospital the girls need to stay quiet. No whooping downstairs like they do here.' She pounded the pastry with a satisfied thump. 'It'll do them all good to get out of the place.' She cast a cautious glance at Kirsty. 'Mind, what the man really needs is a wife. But we're not expecting miracles.'

'I wouldn't expect miracles either,' Kirsty said flatly. 'The man's a loner.'

'He thinks you're a bit of all right,' Ben piped up from his chasm, and Kirsty winced.

'We all think Kirsty's a bit of all right,' Margie said, casting a severe look at her husband. 'No matchmaking, Ben. You know it only leads to trouble.'

'Trouble's what's life's about,' Ben said, with a satisfied yawn. 'Life's boring without it.'

'Kenneth's trouble,' Margie retorted.

'There's trouble and there's trouble,' Ben said sagely. 'Some comes looking for you and you run a mile. Some you go looking for yourself. I'd reckon our Dr Jake is right in the middle and he doesn't know which is which. And neither do you, miss,' he said obscurely to Kirsty. 'Maybe it'll be fun to stick around for a while and watch.'

To Kirsty's surprise, what followed were a few really restful days.

Jake and his family moved into the castle but, apart from mealtimes, Kirsty hardly saw Jake. OK, she avoided him as much as she could and maybe he was avoiding her. If so, she wasn't asking questions.

Kenneth seemed no trouble at all.

Jake reported that he'd sent him by ambulance him to Melbourne with a request for psychiatric evaluation. The authorities rang back and said that he seemed settled and rational, they could see no reason to hold him and they'd released him with instructions to maintain his medication. For a couple of days they expected him to return breathing fire, but there was no sign of him.

'You could go home again,' Susie told Jake over dinner on the third night, but she said it reluctantly. He heard the reluctance and smiled. He must feel how good this was, Kirsty thought. It was great for all of them. Angus and Susie were almost unrecognisable from the two invalids they'd been only days ago.

'If it's OK with Angus, we might extend our stay for a few more days,' Jake said softly. 'The man still makes me nervous.'

'And your kiddies would be having an excellent time,' Angus said in satisfaction. 'This place sounds as it ought to. Full of noise and life.' He ladled out more of Mrs Boyce's casserole. 'There should be more of it.'

'If you're sure we're not intruding…'

'I'm hardly seeing you, Jake,' Angus said bluntly. 'The kids and the girls and Margie and Ben are intruding all over the place and I love it, but you're never here.'

'I'm working.'

'Let our Kirsty share, then. She's aching to.'

'Kirsty's helping.'

'Not enough,' Angus said bluntly. 'Let her help with clinics.'

'She did inoculations today.'

She had, Kirsty thought. She'd visited the local primary school and administered seventy inoculations. Sure, it had saved Jake a few hours so he could be home earlier to his kids, but it was hardly earth-shattering medicine.

She *could* help in his clinic. Her provisional registration was all in order, but there was a problem. Working in the clinic meant working side by side with Jake, and it made both of them nervous. They'd performed all the outstanding surgery, and now Jake was accepting her help only when it meant they worked apart.

Which was probably just as well, she thought and looked across to where Susie was teasing the twins into eating their vegetables. This was working out better than she'd ever dreamed. If Susie had a few weeks of this before her baby was born, maybe the depression could be put behind her.

Which was the important thing.

She returned her attention to her casserole, but suddenly she was aware that she was being watched.

Susie knew things were wrong. Her twin antennae had her asking questions Kirsty couldn't answer. And Margie and Ben were very astute.

So was Jake. He'd heard the sudden stillness, and he'd heard the unuttered questions.

'I need to go,' he said, pushing his chair back abruptly. He placed a hand on each of his daughter's heads. 'I have evening clinic. Will you let Margie put you to bed?'

'Susie's reading me a story tonight,' Alice told him. 'Kirsty's reading to Penelope. Tomorrow we're going to swap.'

'I can read to both girls if you need Kirsty to help you,' Susie ventured, but Jake was already walking out the door.

'I'm fine alone,' he told them. And went.

The days dragged on. When Jake had said he was fine alone, he meant he was fine alone. It was as if since he'd admitted he needed help he'd backed off and changed his mind.

Between them they'd operated on Dorothy Miller's veins, Mark Glaston's skin cancer and Scotty Anderson's osteochondroma, but they were small operations and all they did was give Kirsty a taste of what she was missing. She offered to do more, but the work Jake offered was minor.

'Your major effort is to keep Angus and Susie healthy,' he told her.

Fine. But Angus and Susie were taking care of each other.

Angus had hardly moved over the past few weeks. With his oxygen levels vastly improved, he was now ambulatory but he was still very shaky. About as shaky as Susie.

So he and Susie organised a track around the vegetable patch, where a railed wall gave them a handhold. Then they set themselves to see who could make it around the patch fastest.

As supervising medical officer, Kirsty was supposed to watch and pick them up if they fell over—but as races went, it would be faster to watch grass grow.

What was wrong with her? Kirsty demanded of herself after a week. Why was she miserable?

She should be happy. Susie was happier and healthier every day. So was Angus. There was no sign of Kenneth. The only reason the castle was still full of people was because everyone acknowledged how wonderful this arrangement was for Angus and Susie. Now the two little girls were tumbling with Boris on the grass in the late afternoon sun. The invalids were practising their walking. Ben had gone home to tend his own vegetable garden. Margie was cooking. Kirsty had a great book to read. God was in his heaven, all was right with her world—and all she could do was think about where Jake was.

She was going nuts.

'I think I'll go out and see Mavis,' she decided when Ben returned and offered to take over race supervision.

'Jake goes there most afternoons,' Ben told her, grinning, but she decided dignity was the only way to react to his teasing.

'If I'm not required, I won't go in,' she said in her very smoothest professional manner.

'You go in, girl, and see her anyway,' Margie said firmly. 'Ben, you keep your nose out of what doesn't concern you.'

'You will watch Susie and Angus?' Kirsty asked, trying to ignore the pair of them. Two identical grins. Drat them.

'It's the tortoise versus the tortoise,' Margie said, looking over to where Angus was considering taking a couple of steps without the rail and thus overtaking Susie. 'How exciting. Of course we'll supervise. Off you go, dear, and see if you can move a little faster than this odd couple. Dinner's in an hour but if you don't get back in time it's no problem. I've made sausage rolls and there's plenty.'

What was wrong with her?

She sat in her car and glowered at her own stupidity. It was a relief to be away from the castle. She needed time. She needed…

She didn't know what she needed.

She slowed down and then pulled off the road to admire the scenery. The views here were fabulous. Dolphins were surfing in the waves just beneath the cliff-side road. That made her glower lessen. She watched in fascinated delight, but then the dolphins gave up on their surfing and disappeared off to wherever dolphins went. Life had to go on.

Mavis. She was going to see Mavis.

But when she reached the farm, Ben was proved right. Jake's car was already there, and her glower sprang right back. Jake should be back at the hospital doing all his very important work that kept him away from the castle all the time, she thought savagely, and then she made a valiant attempt to regain some semblance of professionalism and thought maybe Mavis was in trouble.

And if Mavis was in trouble, then she, as consultant specialist, ought to be in there with her, instead of sitting out here glowering like a lovesick teenager. Her dumb emotions had no basis in logic. She had to stay in this place for a few weeks yet, so she may as well get on with acting normal right now.

Right. Normal.

She headed up the porch steps as Jake came out the front door, and she had to struggle really hard not to start glowering again.

'Hi,' she said, and he looked at her blankly, like he'd forgotten who she was.

'Why are you here?'

'I thought you asked me to stay in touch with Mavis.'

'I did. But I thought you were back at the castle.'

'Well, I'm not,' she said crossly. 'How's our patient?'

'Sitting up in bed with two grandchildren and a paint-a-Rembrandt-by-numbers kit,' he told her, allowing himself to smile. 'There's paint everywhere and Barbara's trying to act crabby. You want to see?'

'I do,' she said, and she even smiled back—but then she remembered who she was talking to and she stopped smiling. 'But I won't keep you. You're obviously busy.'

'Not so busy that I can't enjoy your reaction to what you've done,' he said, standing aside and letting her past. 'You've done great, Dr McMahon.'

She flushed. She had to walk right by him and she flushed some more.

She needed to go back to the States, she thought desperately. She was losing her mind.

But she wasn't losing her touch with her medicine. She walked into Mavis's bedroom and stopped in astonishment.

The room was full of family. Mavis was propped up on pillows, with a grandchild on either side of her. The bed had been pulled out from the wall so the kids could have a chair apiece either side, and they'd added a few books to get the children—a boy and a girl of about five and seven—to the right height. A tray had been set up over Mavis's knees to hold paints and brushes and canvas.

There was as much paint on the bedspread as there was on

the canvas but no one seemed to be minding. Everyone looked up as Kirsty walked in, and everyone smiled. Barbara was by the window, and as she came forward Kirsty saw the faint glimmer of tears on her lashes.

But they weren't tears of despair, she thought. The change in the sickroom since the week before was little short of miraculous. Pain was an absolute killer all by itself. It ruined lives before death. If it could be held at bay…

She'd succeeded. There was no need to ask. It was written all over Mavis's face.

'So you don't need me to adjust anything?' she said softly, doing a fast blink herself. Mavis's smile broadened.

'Oh, no, dear. I'm doing very nicely.'

It would change again, Kirsty thought. This disease was cruel and it was terminal. The bone metastases would be growing and the pain regime would have to be tweaked every day for as long as the old lady had left. But for now she was enjoying life, and Kirsty could keep tweaking the pain regimen.

Kirsty could keep tweaking until Susie delivered her baby and she left.

'You'll train me before you go,' Jake said softly, and she knew he was thinking the same thing. And it slammed into her all over again—that Jake seemed somehow to share her thinking. The knowledge was extraordinarily intimate. More, it was just plain extraordinary. She saw him smile, and she wondered how it was that she could meet such a man when he wasn't interested. When she lived half a world away. When she didn't want involvement. When the whole thing was ridiculous.

And she wondered whether he knew she was thinking that, too.

'Of course I'll run through the latest pain management regimen for this sort of disease with you,' she said, a trifle distractedly. She managed to smile at Mavis and turned determinedly away from Jake. 'Can I interrupt the painting to do a quick check? Do you have any sore spots?'

'My hip's bothering me a little,' Mavis admitted. 'But it's so much better than last week that I don't like to complain.'

'The squeaky wheel gets the oil,' Kirsty told her, still trying her best to ignore Jake. If dumb platitudes filled the uneasy silence, then he'd get dumb platitudes, but platitudes weren't going to stop her being acutely aware of him every minute. 'Dr Cameron, why don't you take these two aspiring artists for a walk?' she said desperately. 'Then their grandma and I can have a discussion about a sore hip.'

She could still help. Once Jake left she relaxed. Not only did she assist Mavis with her hip pain, she spent some time talking about the future, reassuring the old lady that the pain could be kept at bay for as long as it took.

'We may have to change the cocktail over and over again,' she told her. 'But we can. Even when I go, I'll leave instructions as to what to do in the future, and I'm always on the end of the phone. And Dr Cameron is good. He was about to phone for help from a city pain specialist when I arrived, and if I leave he'll still do that.'

'I wish you could stay,' Mavis said wistfully, but Kirsty thought there might well be six months or so left to the old lady—maybe even more—and she could make no promises.

The sun was losing its warmth when she left. She checked her watch and realised she'd dawdled too long on the way there. They were expecting her back at the castle for dinner.

But when she went out to the veranda there was another patient lined up. Jake was sitting on the veranda steps with a farmer by the looks of him, a man in his sixties or early seventies. The man glanced up at her, grinned, a gap-toothed grin in a battered and not-so-clean face.

'This'll be the other doc,' he said in satisfaction. 'Two for the price of one. Barbara said Doc'd be coming tonight and I watched the road for his car. Now I have the pair of you.'

'Herbert lives just over the rise,' Jake said dryly, with a look that was almost apologetic. 'Herbert, this is Dr McMahon. Herbert doesn't like clinic because he doesn't like waiting.'

'The missus makes me have a bath before I go to clinic. A man could waste a whole day on a visit like that,' Herbert said indignantly. 'Me leg's a bit of a mess and the missus said she'd drag me in tomorrow regardless. But now I've found you…' He beamed. 'If you could just fix me up.'

He hauled up his trouser leg and revealed a gory haematoma, with a long jagged gash in the centre. There were angry red weals leading up the leg toward the groin. It didn't take a brains trust to realise this injury had taken place some days before and had been ignored.

'So what happened?' Jake asked. They had an audience. Barbara was standing watching, holding a child by each hand. These were farm kids, Kirsty thought in wry amusement. A kid from Manhattan might well faint, but all these children showed was fascinated interest.

'Blasted heifer kicked out as I was putting her into a bail last Monday,' Herbert said sourly. 'It was her first time in. I should know better by now and keep myself out of the way, but I'm getting slower in my old age. Anyway, the missus saw it last night and had a pink fit and said the leg'd drop off if I didn't see you. So I'm seeing you.'

'I don't suppose there's any chance you might come to the hospital,' Jake said, but he sounded amused more than annoyed and he didn't look surprised when Herbert shook his head.

'The leg'll have to turn black before that happens.'

'The leg may well turn black if you don't take more care of it,' Jake said bluntly. He looked up at Barbara. 'Is it OK if Dr McMahon and I perform a piece of minor surgery on your veranda?'

'It's Mum's veranda,' Barbara said. She smiled and motioned to where her mother was watching through the bedroom window. 'As long as you don't mind an audience, go right ahead.'

* * *

This was seriously weird, Kirsty decided.

Jake propped the farmer on cushions. He spread newspapers under his leg and asked Kirsty to administer a full shin block. Then he proceeded to clean the wound of accumulated debris— of which there was plenty—getting rid of the dead flaps of torn skin and checking the circulation around the wound. Dirty wounds were best left open as much as possible. They both knew that to Herbert cosmetic appearances were a very minor consideration, but the tear was big and Jake needed to pull it together with a few stitches.

The kids watched. A couple of hens clucked past, and all the while Herbert lay back and discussed the state of the poddy market with Barbara.

'Those damned Friesians of mine only got fifty quid last week,' he complained. 'You and your old man got seventy.'

'That's because we feed 'em right,' Barbara said severely. 'You're too much of a skinflint to give them what they need, and whoever buys them has to go into TLC mode.'

'What's TLC?'

'Tender loving care,' Barbara retorted. 'Something you ought to have used on your leg, you dopey git.'

There was a wealth of affection between them, Kirsty realised, and then she thought, more—there was a wealth of affection within this whole community. Jake cared for all these people. They cared for Jake and they cared for each other. He was right. This was the best community in which to raise kids.

What if Susie wanted to stay here after the baby was born? What was she thinking that for? Why would Susie want to stay?

Why would she want to go home?

Not for family, Kirsty thought ruefully. They had no one but each other.

But here…here Susie had Angus and the Boyces and Jake and a vegetable garden and people who were prepared to love her.

Maybe Susie might want to stay.

Which left Kirsty where?

Home was where the heart was. Another platitude. She was getting good at platitudes.

So what did she have back in Manhattan to tug at her heart? Who did she have?

Robert?

Ha.

Oh, stop it, she told herself fiercely as she watched Jake dress the farmer's leg. You're being maudlin.

She'd go back to the castle right now, she decided. Jake put on a last piece of sticking plaster. She administered a dose of intravenous antibiotic with care and rose to leave. Her work here was done.

'Surgery tomorrow morning at nine to have this checked,' Jake was telling Herbert.

'Aw, Doc, you know I don't have time to come to surgery.'

'I'll ring Maudie and tell her to tip out your stock of home-brewed if you're not there,' he retorted, as the farmer struggled to his feet as well. The downside of using the veranda floor as an operating table was that patient access wasn't so great. Jake took one arm and Kirsty the other. Herbert was a bit wobbly. He reached into his pocket for his car keys but Barbara was before him, darting forward and snatching them from his hand.

'I'll call Sam from the dairy to take you home,' Barbara said. 'Milking's finished. He won't mind.' As he opened his mouth to argue she took a couple of steps backward with the keys. 'You and Maudie can pick up your car after the doctor's surgery tomorrow, and if Maudie doesn't tell me you've been looking after yourself, you're not getting your keys back at all.'

The farmer glowered, but only for a minute. His glower slowly faded and became a rueful grin.

'Dratted women,' he told Jake. 'You know what you're doing, not getting leg-shackled again.' He cast an appraising look at Kirsty. 'Though from what I hear, you'd better look out.'

'I will,' Jake said, and Kirsty released the farmer's arm as if it burned.

'Though she's a looker,' Herbert said, grinning.

'Do you mind?' she said faintly.

'Not a bit,' Herbert said, his grin broadening. 'I can see what they're talking about now.'

There was a choking sound from Barbara.

'Now, don't get offended,' Barbara begged. 'You can't hold it against Herbert—or any of us, for that matter. This district has been matchmaking for Dr Jake for years. We just have to set eyes on an eligible woman and we're at it. Indulge us.'

So maybe Jake had his reasons for saying he wasn't wanting a relationship up front, Kirsty thought, a flash of sympathy filtering though her anger.

'I'm not offended,' she managed. 'Just bemused that you can think anything so ridiculous.'

'Ridiculous is this district's specialty,' Jake said wryly, but then his cell phone rang. 'Dammit, please, let this not be more work.'

She should take this chance to leave, Kirsty thought. She should. But she hesitated just a moment too long.

'You're kidding,' Jake was saying into the phone. 'How can you do that? It's almost grounds for dismissal without a reference.' He heaved a doleful sigh.

'Fine, then,' he said, even more dolefully. 'We'll just starve. No, no, think nothing of it. We'll fade to shadows of our former selves, but we'll fade as martyrs.'

He replaced the phone on his belt and found them all looking at him.

'It's a tragedy,' he said, still doleful.

'Tragedy?' Kirsty asked, cautious. His eyes were twinkling in that dangerous way he had that said there was no tragedy at all.

'Angus and Susie are feeling better.'

'Um…that's a tragedy?' She didn't want to ask, Kirsty decided. But his eyes were laughing openly, even though his mouth was trying to be tragic. He had her intrigued.

'Mrs Boyce has made soup and sausage rolls for dinner,' he said sadly. 'Everyone's been exercising, they were hungry and we're late. She couldn't make them wait for us and I'm sorry to have to inform you, Kirsty, that they've eaten the lot.' His face grew even more mournful. 'Which leaves you and me with no dinner. Margie says we need to buy fish and chips on the way home.'

'Have something here,' Barbara said, and hesitated. 'I can stretch...'

Country hospitality at its best, Kirsty thought. This lady was managing kids, a farm and a dying mother, and she still offered to feed all comers.

'Margie can give us eggs on toast,' Jake said, sighing his martyred sigh again. 'But no.' He held up a hand to stop Barbara's protest. 'Dr McMahon and I are true medical heroes. We know how to exist on a piece of stale bread and dripping and tea made with a used teabag. Fish and chips will be sheer luxury.'

'Have it on the beach,' Herbert said approvingly. 'Just like me and the missus. We take a bottle of wine down there every Friday night, and nine times out of ten it ends up in a spot of hanky-panky.' He suddenly realised what he was saying and gave an embarrassed snort. 'I mean...when we were younger it ended up in hanky-panky.' His colour deepened as he realised they were all looking at him, fascinated. 'In the old days. I mean...'

Ooh, sexy, Kirsty thought. Fish and chips and hanky-panky with Herbert.

'That sounds just what you both need,' Mavis volunteered from her window behind them. 'If I was forty years younger, I'd join you.'

Fish and chips and hanky-panky with Herbert and Mavis, too?

Or just fish and chips with Jake. On the beach.

Where was she going? Into territory that was very dangerous indeed.

'We'll buy fish and chips and take them home,' Kirsty said, a trifle desperately, but Barbara shook her head.

'I can guess what'll happen if you do that, and I bet you can, too. They'll all have had sausage rolls, and they'll be as full as googs, but you step inside the castle with fish and chips and suddenly they'll be hungry all over again. They'll be gone in a flash, mark my words. You take her down the beach, Dr Jake.'

'Yeah, Dr Jake,' Herbert said, and nudged Jake in the ribs. 'Take her down the beach.'

'I don't need fish and chips,' Kirsty said, with an attempt at dignity, but she was howled down by everyone.

Except maybe Jake? But Jake said nothing as plans were made around them. As they were told sternly what to do.

'You are hungry?' Jake asked as silence finally reigned, and she had to agree that she was.

'Right, then,' he said with resignation. 'It's fish and chips on the beach. By order.'

And five minutes later she was meekly following Jake's car to the Dolphin Bay fish and chippery—and to the beach beyond.

CHAPTER SEVEN

WHILE Jake purchased fish and chips, Kirsty walked across the park separating the town from the beach. The park was a gorgeous little triangle—beach on one side, river with harbour on another and the town on the third side. It was a great little town, Kirsty thought, falling deeper in love with this strange mix of bushland and harbour and sleepy village.

There was a pair of kookaburras in the gums above her head. Their mocking chortles made her feel weird. She shouldn't be here. Why was she here?

They both knew this was dangerous territory.

Oh, for heaven's sake, this was fish and chips on the beach-front. It wasn't one of Jake's scary dates. It was…nothing.

Safe or not, Kirsty found a table close to the shops—just *because*—but then Jake strolled up bearing a fat parcel of fish and chips and a couple of bottles of lemonade. He smiled as he put his load on the table and she didn't feel safe at all.

'We should take these home,' she managed, but Jake's smile became rueful.

'Barbara's right. The scavengers would have it in minutes and I'm starving.'

So was she. When he ripped the paper to reveal slivers of flathead, tiny, succulent scallops, fresh oysters and enough chips to feed a small army, she decided that no way was she taking this home.

'This is my half,' she said, putting a hand through the halfway mark, hauling her fish, chips, scallops and oysters to her side of the paper and thus delineating shares.

'Hey,' he said, startled. 'I thought women were supposed to pretend they didn't eat.'

'Not this woman. I've been watching Susie peck at her food for months now. She gags at the sight of anything fried so we've been having healthy little morsels of not very much at all. To have a nice carbohydrate-loaded meal in front of me—where I have to fight for every mouthful—is the stuff of dreams.'

'I'm happy to oblige,' he said, but he still looked disbelieving and Kirsty was aware that she was being watched all the time she ate.

'What?' she said at last as the final scallop found a thoroughly satisfactory home. 'You look like you've never seen anyone eat a chip before. You must have.'

'I've never seen anyone like you.'

'Watch Susie, then. She's identical.'

'She's not identical.'

'Because she's pregnant and battered? She'll recover. But she'll be a stronger person than I'll ever be,' Kirsty agreed.

'You mean because life's tossed her around?' he asked curiously. 'You don't think you might be just as strong?'

'I'm not strong.'

'When I rang to check on your credentials for registration, I got a glowing report,' he said. 'Smart, caring, ambitious and poised to become one of the youngest-ever medical directors of the hospice you've been working in. Strong was one of the biggest words they used. You have the reputation for fighting with everything you have to see your patients get what they need to make them comfortable to the end. It's a hugely prestigious establishment, and to have the credentials to take over at your age seems amazing.' He paused. 'But then you walked away,' he said softly. 'You haven't been near the place for the last three months and the appointment's been given to someone else.'

'There's lots of jobs,' she said a trifle self-consciously. 'It's no big deal.'

'The woman I talked to said it was a big deal. A really big deal. In the cutthroat medical establishment, for you to walk away because you cared so much for your sister is tantamount to professional suicide.'

'That's nonsense,' she said, suddenly angry. He was intruding on her personal space here—her personal doubts? 'Oh, maybe it's the truth in a sense—to get where I was headed you need to be blinkered to everything else in the world. Maybe I was for a while but maybe being blinkered is dumb. Family comes first.'

'My ex-wife's still dumb,' he said inconsequentially, and for some reason that made her angrier.

'Good for her, then. Each to his own and every other platitude I can think of.' She rose and stalked over to the nearest rubbish bin, depositing her empty wrappings with force.

'Um…platitudes?' he said cautiously, and she shook her head without turning back to him.

'Don't ask. I'm going for a walk on the beach. You go on home.'

'You're dismissing me?'

'I am,' she told him. 'If we're seen walking on the beach together in this town, I don't think we need a wedding certificate. It'll be seen as a done deal.'

He grinned at that. 'You're starting to see what I'm up against.'

'Maybe,' she conceded. 'But you weren't polite.'

'I've forgotten how to be polite.'

'Sure.' She'd reached the sand and was hauling off her sandals, then rolling up her jeans. When she straightened she found he was beside her, doing the same.

'You're supposed to be going home.'

'The kids ate my sausage rolls. They all ate our sausage rolls. There's no bedtime story for sausage-roll eaters.'

'What you mean is that they won't even notice that you're

not there,' she said, softening. 'There are people queued for bedtime reading rights. You've made so many people happy by lending us your family.'

'Good old Kenneth,' he said softly. 'He doesn't know what he's started.'

'I suppose it was Kenneth that pulled everyone together,' she said. 'You'll have to forget him soon though, and let everyone go home.'

'Who wants to go home?' he said enigmatically. 'I'm for walking on the beach. How about you?'

'Different sides of the beach?' she said cautiously.

'Of course. You want me to go get Boris to chaperon?'

'We should.'

'If I went and got him then everyone would come back and join us.'

'Which would make this a really big deal,' she said softly. 'And we don't want that, do we, Dr Cameron?'

In the end it was a really long walk. She'd been strained to the limit, Kirsty thought as they walked. Maybe ever since Rory had died. Caring for Susie, trying to juggle her work commitments, trying to figure out the best for everyone had taken all her mental energy. Even the time of enforced idleness in Sydney while Susie had been threatened with early birth had been frighteningly tense—watching Susie's depression increase, knowing how helpless she was.

But this last week had been a gift for her, too, she decided as she walked. She wasn't the least sure what sort of emotional jumble her head was in, but for the rest…she'd relaxed about Susie. There was now only three weeks to go. The baby could be born now and be safe.

As well as that, she'd practised medicine again. It was an odd sort of general practice—anaesthetics, pain management and the odds and sods that Jake didn't want. But it had been fun giving assorted schoolkids their shots, watching them screw up their faces in terror and offer their bare arms like lambs to the slaughter—only to be astounded when she'd managed to give the shot with hardly a pinprick of pain.

She'd also had fun at the castle. Kenneth's threats had become a catalyst to make everyone seem a family and…

And for the first time in a very long time she'd seemed part of a family. Most of that was because of the man beside her.

It was no wonder that her hormones were playing tricks on her, she thought dimly, and then she thought it didn't help that he was so drop-dead gorgeous and he was so drop-dead caring and he was so drop-dead…everything.

'Penny for your thoughts,' Jake said, and she jerked out of her reverie, surprised to see they'd walked almost half a mile. They'd been walking in the shallows, separated by a few feet so the splashes she was making didn't hit him and vice versa.

'I'm just thinking this has been fun,' she told him.

'Fun?'

'Giving kids shots. Watching Angus and Susie have races. Bouncing around the castle with Boris and Penelope and Alice.'

'They've had fun, too.' They paused. The sun was a vast, golden ball dropping low over the distant mountains, slipping every moment until, pop, it suddenly disappeared altogether, leaving only the glorious hues of sunset. 'We'd better go back.'

They turned but he seemed as reluctant as she was.

Silence again. Why didn't he talk? she wondered. He acted as if he was afraid of her.

'So you're never going to have a relationship again?' she asked softly, and the silence intensified.

'Sorry?' she said at last. 'I didn't hear your answer.'

'I was trying not to hear your question.'

'I'm allowed to ask,' she said, a trifle indignantly. 'After all, remember hubby and the six kidlets back home.'

'I'd forgotten them,' he said, starting to smile. 'Maybe because you don't wear photos of them in a locket round your neck.'

'Too many,' she said sagely. 'I'd get a sore neck.'

'But if you did, it'd stop the locals talking about us,' Jake told her.

'That really gets to you.'

'It does,' he agreed. 'Every single woman in this place seems at some time or other to be bracketed with me. It gets tiring.'

'I'd imagine it would,' she said faintly. 'All those women.'

'It's just…' He kicked spray up before him with a sudden savage swipe that had his pants and shirt covered with spray. No problem, Kirsty thought. The unseasonable cold snap as they'd arrived had lasted a whole three minutes and it was now back to late-summer gorgeous. He'd dry before they reached the end of the beach. 'Look, the small-town thing is dumb. It's why I came here—because everyone cares for everyone—and this is just its downside so I shouldn't complain.'

'Why do you care what they say?' she asked cautiously. 'Is it so important? If someone sees you kissing someone else and sets it about that you're having a hot affair—is that such a tragedy?'

'My kids.'

'It's hardly going to affect your kids,' she said, with more asperity than she'd intended. 'They're four years old. They're hardly likely to be corrupted.'

'But if the woman gets the wrong idea…'

'You're scared that touching a woman leads to immediate presumption of marriage. You know, that does seem a trifle… presumptuous.'

'It does,' he said, giving her a rueful smile. 'It sounds conceited.'

'It definitely does.'

'So if I kissed you, you wouldn't think it'd lead anywhere.'

She thought about that. 'I guess it couldn't,' she agreed cautiously. 'On account of hubby and rug-rats back home.'

He motioned up to the headland. There was a car park overlooking the harbour, a place Kirsty had discovered was a favourite with the locals. They drove up there at odd times in the day just to check to the state of surf, the tides, whether the fishing fleet was in sight. At any time of the day there were never less than half a dozen cars parked there, and now Kirsty could count at least ten.

'You know,' Kirsty said cautiously, 'if you were to kiss me now, you could use it as armour for years.'

'How so?' They'd slowed, and now they stopped, ankle deep in the surf.

'It'd be all over town by morning. Doctor has passionate affair with other doctor. Then nothing. Doctor goes back to New York, leaving bereft country doctor behind. You could hide behind your broken heart for ages.'

'Gee, thanks.'

'Just a thought,' she said, and grinned. 'Just offering myself in the greater good. If you need armour, what better than a broken heart? Or...' She paused. 'I could tell everyone you knew about hubby and the six kids. That'd work. Maybe it'd even work better.'

'How would it work better?' He was staring at her as if she'd grown antennae.

'Mothers would warn their daughters about you. Don't go near him, dear, he's a home-wrecker.'

'You've got it all worked out.'

'Just trying to be helpful.'

'Why?'

'You're miserable,' she told him. 'I'm a pain specialist. Fixing pain is what I do.'

'What makes you think I'm in pain?'

'I think you're lonely as hell,' she said bluntly. 'I think your wife walking out on you has left you bewildered and hurt and scared. You want to keep you and your two little girls safe from being hurt again, and you're using local gossip as an excuse not to let anyone close.'

'That's nonsense.'

'Is it?' She turned to face him then, head on. 'Is it really, Jake? It's partly what you told me. We'd hardly met before you were telling me to back off, and you know there's a solid mutual attraction. Fictional kidlets aside, is there really a sensible reason why you're not kissing me now? When you know we both want to?'

'I…'

She raised her brows in mock enquiry and turned away, taking a few more steps in the shallows. Was she mad? Solitude and fear over the last month had driven her to the edge, she thought, and any minute she'd be declared as crazed as Kenneth.

And then she heard Jake splash behind her.

She paused, not knowing whether she should be hopeful or not. But she *was* hopeful.

'Kirsty?'

'Yes?'

'It's either kiss you or throttle you,' he told her, sounding much more exasperated than passionate. 'So turn around and be kissed.'

He kissed her.

He was crazy. This was dumb. She'd goaded him into it and it made all the sense in the world to walk away, but she was too…

Too Kirsty.

It stunned him. She'd walked into his life and something had lit that hadn't been lit for years—if it ever had been lit, and somehow he doubted it. He'd thought he'd been in love when he'd married, but he hadn't felt like this.

Like he was balancing on a knife-edge.

She'd accused him of being scared, he thought, and she was right. Ever since he'd been left with two babies to make a future for, every decision had been carefully controlled. But Kirsty was uncontrolled. Uncontrollable.

Kirsty.

This was madness. This was not a sensible move at all, but she was right before him, her eyes wide with gentle, mocking enquiry. A man could drown in those eyes. A man could lose control completely. No, it wasn't the least bit sensible but she was waiting to be kissed. The watchers on the clifftop were waiting for a man to kiss a woman. Kirsty had defied him to put on a show for their audience, and suddenly he couldn't help himself.

And when he took her hands in his, when he drew her to him and kissed her, softly, wonderingly on the mouth, it was like the coming together of two halves of a whole.

She was so...right!

He'd thought he'd known how a woman felt—of course he did—but this was different. Each curve; the soft warmth of her; every part of her moulding against him, fitting with a completeness that was as shocking as it was wonderful.

He knew this woman, he thought numbly. He'd always known her, but he hadn't found her until now. And then he stopped thinking anything at all as his mind shuttered down and all he felt was the kiss.

And Kirsty...

Kirsty had goaded him into this kiss, half laughing, but half of her desperately wanting. It was as if she'd been defying herself to find that it couldn't be as wonderful as her subconscious was screaming that it could be. But her subconscious had been overwhelmingly, deliciously right.

Her hands came up to cup his face, deepening the kiss, and she felt the rough beginning of stubble on his tough male skin. It was so erotic she felt her toes start to curl.

She'd kissed men. Of course she'd kissed men.

Nobody had caused her toes to curl as this man was doing right now.

And she could keep kissing him. It was unbelievable that he was kissing her, that she was holding him and he wasn't pulling away, that he was deepening the kiss, seemingly wanting her as much as she wanted him.

Nothing had ever felt so right. Her breasts were against his chest, his hands were tugging her waist, drawing her into him, and she was arching against him. Aching. Loving. Welcoming her man to her, as a woman welcomed her man home after battle.

Home to her heart.

This couldn't last. They were playing for an audience, she thought in the tiny recess of her brain still available for anything but pure, hot sensation. In a moment he'd pull away and all the reasons why he didn't want a relationship, why she didn't want a relationship, would surface and life would go on as before.

This was time out for both of them but she wasn't going to stop it. To do so would be dumb, and she didn't feel dumb. She felt light and hot and wonderful and…loved.

Loved?

Maybe she was dumb after all. Her hands moved to pull him closer, tighter, to deepen the kiss as if to block out the unwanted intrusion of sanity.

But it had happened and maybe he'd felt it, or maybe he'd had his own intrusive thoughts because suddenly he was pulling away. His hands caught hers, using them to hold her away from him. Just a little.

His eyes were quizzical, laughing—but she was starting to know this man and she could see uncertainty behind the façade of laughter.

'Do you think that's given them enough?'

'No,' she said, trying to match his laughter. But she was aware that the unsteadiness of her voice must be a give-away to the jumble of emotions within. 'They won't be satisfied unless you rip my clothes off and take me, right here.'

'You want to do that?' he asked, the smile still managing to stay—but both of them knew that what he was suggesting was entirely possible, given another time, another place…

Another life.

He released her hands and it was all she could do not to cry. Such a loss.

'Maybe being known as Dolphin Bay's town slut isn't quite

what I had in mind,' she managed, still trying for lightness. 'Though it'd do wonders for your reputation. Fornication in public? No mother in her right mind would let her daughter so much as come to you for a flu jab.'

'Then maybe we'd better not.'

'Maybe we'd better not.'

He caught her hand again, simply, girl to boy, swinging her around so they were side by side, facing the cliff. It was a simple gesture, but the feel of his fingers entwined in hers moved her unutterably. She glanced up at the line of cars, trying to take her mind off the feel of his hand. By the time they reached the car park their audience would have completely dispersed, she decided. The town gossip network was about to move into meltdown.

'You think what we've just done will keep me safe from matchmaking?' Jake murmured, and the lightness had suddenly gone from his voice. His fingers were gripping hers with force as well as with warmth.

'For the next few weeks they'll bracket us together,' she whispered. 'Everyone knows we've been sleeping in the same castle. The local gossip lines will all but self-destruct. Then when I go you can be heartbroken all over again, just as you were when your wife left. Getting over your wife has given you years of grace. The town is only starting to gear up seriously to matchmake. And now you've another lost love.'

'You're my lost love,' he said, sounding startled.

'I make a good one, don't you think?'

'Um…sure.'

'There you go, then.' She was working so hard on keeping it light that something inside her was threatening to break. She was so close to tears…

There was a ring from his shirt pocket and she thought, Thank heaven for cell phones. Anything to break this moment. Anything to give her space. She walked away a little, and she could almost hear the collective sigh of disappointment from the clifftop.

Could she stand living here as the local doctor and being watched every day?

Maybe not. Not unless…

Don't go there, she told herself. She shrugged and hiked up the beach, and by the time Jake reached her she was sitting on the sand, pulling her sandals back on. Their time of make-believe was over.

'They were lovely fish and chips,' she told him, trying to sound polite and dismissive. 'It was a very nice walk and a very nice kiss. Thank you very much, Doctor.'

His lips twitched. 'Just like that? Consultation over?'

'I'd be guessing you have places to go, people to see.'

'Emily Cannon has croup.'

'There you go, then. I'll see you back at home.' Hardly, she thought. Jake and his twins were sleeping in a guest suite on the first floor near Angus, about as far from her as it was possible to be. 'Unless you need help with croup,' she added, trying not to sound hopeful.

'Croup hardly needs a specialist anaesthetist.'

'I still remember croup training.'

'I don't need you.'

You couldn't get more of a dismissal than that. Right.

'Goodnight, then, Dr Cameron,' she told him.

'Goodnight, Dr McMahon.'

'I'd shake hands but our audience seems to have disappeared,' she said, motioning to the deserted car park. 'It'd be a waste of human contact, don't you think?'

But she didn't wait to find out whether he agreed or not. She turned and stalked back to her car with all the dignity a woman could muster.

Which wasn't very much at all.

CHAPTER EIGHT

It WAS a long night. Kirsty lay awake and wondered what on earth she'd done. She'd tossed her dignity aside and behaved like a twit. She'd thrown herself at the man.

'I had fun,' she told herself, trying desperately to lighten what had happened in her head. 'And he had fun, too. We were a mature man and woman play-acting for the local gossips.

'That might be what Jake was doing, but it was far more than play-acting for you, and you know it.'

Sleep wouldn't come. She rose and padded softly into Susie's room, as she'd done so often over the last week, and she found her sister staring at the ceiling as well.

'What's up?' she asked, and Susie turned and smiled at her in the moonlight.

'Nothing's up, stoopid. That's the problem.'

'Huh?'

'I was woken by Rory junior practising his gridiron,' she said. 'Then I had to get up for a pee for the fourth time tonight. And now...I've just been lying here thinking that life suddenly seems hopeful again. Just a little bit,' she said hastily, as if her sister might read too much into her confession. 'But these last days...it's been like slivers of light breaking through fog. Just glimpses, but they're getting longer.'

'That's great,' Kirsty said warmly, perched on her twin's bed. 'Depression is such a ghastly illness. I've been so frightened for you.' She lifted her sister's hand and squeezed. 'I guess I still am.'

'You're thinking the clouds will re-form,' Susie whispered. 'I'm afraid they might, too. It's great that I'm having this…this little bit of happiness but then I remember that Rory isn't here to share it with me. He won't see his baby. Then I think I've got no right to go on.'

Kirsty had left the door open. Angus left a nightlight on—actually a night chandelier—and now a shadow crossed the door. Susie's eyes flew to see who it was, and she smiled a welcome.

'Jake.'

Jake paused in the doorway. Boris was by his side, wagging his tail in greeting. He'd obviously been waiting in the hall for Jake to return and now his tail was sweeping his pleasure.

'Susie.' Jake's voice was warm and caring. 'Is anything wrong?' Then he saw Kirsty, and his voice changed. 'Sorry. You have your personal physician in attendance already. I'm on my way to bed. Come on, Boris.'

'Come in and join us,' Susie called.

Kirsty thought, Rats. But it was callous to say *rats* so she calmly moved up the bed a bit so Jake could come in and sit down.

He came instead to stand, looking searchingly down at Susie. Ignoring Kirsty.

'You really are all right?'

'I really am,' Susie told him. 'And tomorrow Angus and I have organised to see the physiotherapist you told me about.'

That was a huge step forward, Kirsty acknowledged. Up until now Susie had resisted all attempts to get her moving. But Jake had talked about the physiotherapist who visited town once a week. He'd told Angus Susie would benefit, but she wouldn't go by herself—and then he'd told Susie that physiotherapy could prolong Angus's life but he wouldn't go by himself either. Hey, presto, problem fixed. Together they'd go. Country doctor doing what he did best. Sorting out a multitude of problems with interlacing solutions.

Up until now Boris had been standing by Susie's bed. But Kirsty had made room for Jake; the spot was vacant and a dog could only stand temptation for so long. He leapt up, realised how comfortable it was and wriggled forward on his stomach until he was near enough to give Susie a long, slurpy kiss.

'Urk,' Susie said—and giggled.

It was the best sound, Kirsty thought. It was an amazing sound. No matter what sort of emotional mess this man was making of her head, she forgave him all because he'd made her sister giggle.

It had to continue, she thought desperately. But would it? After the baby's birth, hormonal changes could propel her further downward, postnatal depression mingling with an existing diagnosis.

'Susie's feeling guilty that she's started to have glimmers of enjoyment,' she told Jake, jumping in feet first. 'Rory's not here to share it. She's feeling dreadful that she's here and he's not, and she's scared the depression's going to descend again.'

'It's an awful feeling,' Jake said softly. 'I know when my sister died, that was one of the hardest things to come to terms with.'

'Your sister died?' Susie asked. Kirsty didn't say anything. It was like he poleaxed her every time he opened his mouth.

'Car accident when she was sixteen,' he said briefly. 'The first time I forgot…my friends dragged me out to a movie and it was a silly, dopey movie where we all ended up drunk on laughter and life and sheer teenage silliness. And I came out into the night and thought, Elly's never going to see that movie. It was so gut-wrenching that I threw up. My body reacted to mental anguish by physical revolt.'

'Your friends wouldn't have understood,' Susie whispered.

'I told them I had a stomach upset,' he told them. 'Maybe they believed me. They probably did, come to think of it, as how can you know what loss feels like until you've experienced it? What followed then was months of pseudo-stomach upsets, and even now I have moments. But I've learned…' He hesitated, glancing at Kirsty as if unsure that he should reveal himself so completely in her presence. 'But I've learned that I can't not see movies. Or go to the beach, or have my twenty-first birthday or get married and have kids just to stop my gut wrenching. Because it doesn't help. Grief and loss twists your gut into such a knot that every now and then you just have to let go, let it all out, sob or vomit or kick inanimate objects or whatever you find helps—but you have to do it. If you don't you stay permanently twisted inside.'

'I guess that's what I have been,' Susie whispered. 'Twisted inside.'

'Just a little bit battered,' he told her, smiling. 'Not so twisted as you'd noticed. Your walking is going great. Rory would be so proud of you.'

'He would, wouldn't he?' she said, a trifle defiantly. And then she looked from Jake to Kirsty and back again. 'So tonight, on the beach—'

'I need to go to bed,' Jake said, cutting her off. 'I've only just got home. Three house-calls in a row and it's two a.m.'

'Tonight on the beach, were you trying to forget something?' Susie said, deliberately and slowly. 'Or were you both truly moving on?'

'I'm not sure what you mean,' Jake said, and cast a glance at Kirsty that accused her of going straight home to her sister and telling all.

Susie caught the glance and smiled.

'Leave her alone. She hasn't said a word. But Margie's sister-in-law was in the car park and the phones have been running hot since. Margie popped in before she went to bed to ask what did I think and wouldn't it be lovely?' Her smile was tentative but it stayed fixed. 'It's only fair to warn you. I'm simply the first to ask the question.'

'Well, you've asked it,' Jake said, with another doubtful look at Kirsty. 'Now I'm going to bed. Goodnight.'

'You haven't answered my question,' Susie complained.

'It's none of your business.'

That was blunt, Kirsty thought, a bit shocked, but Susie's smile peeped out again.

'No. But I'm Kirsty's twin. I know all her nearest and dearest concerns. Ask your own two if you don't believe me. How many secrets do Alice and Penelope keep from each other?'

No, but I don't know the answer to this one, Kirsty thought desperately, and she glanced at her twin and she saw that Susie knew this, too. And maybe that was why she was asking.

'I have one set of twins in my life,' Jake said, and there was a trace of desperation in his voice as he responded. 'I can't cope with two.'

'Cut it out, Suze,' Kirsty said, and there was even more desperation in her tone. 'Let the man go to bed.'

'Only asking,' Susie responded, her intelligent eyes moving from one to the other. She hesitated. 'Has Kirsty told you about her shadows?'

'No…'

'Our mother died when we were ten,' Susie told him. 'Our father suicided soon after. Since then, Kirsty's taken on the cares of the world. She's looked after me—protected me. She's taken on her job at the hospice, taking care of the dying, and I'm sure that's more of the same. Our father suicided because he couldn't move on. I ventured out again and got hit hard. Kirsty's watched from the sidelines and she's decided she doesn't ever want to go there.'

'Cut it out,' Kirsty said with desperation, and Susie smiled.

'You can't have it both ways, kid. You've worked on getting me better and now I am—or a bit. For the first time since Rory died I'm popping my head up from under the fog and taking notice of what's going on around me. The gut twisting isn't happening and I'm feeling…light. And very, very interested in what's happening to my twin.'

'That's good,' Jake said, but he was edging backwards. 'I need to go.'

'Of course you do,' Susie told him. 'Kirsty, you need to go, too.'

'I'm staying for a bit.'

'I don't need you.'

'Yes, you do,' Kirsty snapped. 'Goodnight, Dr Cameron.'

'Goodnight, Dr McMahon.'

And he was gone.

With the door closed safely behind him, Kirsty turned on her twin with a mixture of indignation, anger and shock. 'How could you? Susie, you've scared the man witless. You've scared me witless.'

'You're not scared witless,' Susie said thoughtfully. 'Oh, Kirsty, he's gorgeous. And you kissed him.'

'We were messing around. Having a lend of the locals.'

'Truly?'

'Truly.'

'So,' she said, fixing her twin with a look Kirsty hadn't seen for a long time, 'you're saying you're not in love with Jake Cameron.'

'You're delusional,' Kirsty said. 'I'll take your blood pressure.'

'There's nothing wrong with my blood pressure,' Susie murmured. 'Yours, on the other hand… Ooh, Kirsty, what are you going to tell Robert?'

'Nothing.'

'I don't expect you need to,' she said thoughtfully. 'He's so limp he's not even likely to notice he's been dumped.'

'Suze!'

'Get out of it,' Susie told her twin. 'Off you go. Leave me to my dreams. But something tells me they're not all dreams. You can't be a twin without knowing a thing or two, and I know a thing or six!'

How was a girl supposed to sleep after that?

She hardly did. She woke up early, and decided she'd make herself breakfast. But when she reached the kitchen door she heard Jake's voice and paused.

'We've got to get you fat somehow,' he was saying. 'An accompanying bag of bones does nothing for my medical image. If you want to be a super-doctor's dog, you need to look a walking advertisement for vitamin pills. Have another rasher.'

Jake and Boris.

She leaned back against the wall, unashamedly eavesdropping.

'We have to go home soon, mate. We're only here in protection mode and it seems there's no threat.'

There was a faint whimper and she could imagine Boris's dopey ears sprawled over Jake's knee.

'Yeah, it's been good. But to pretend it could be like this all the time is dumb. Happy families are an illusion.'

Another whimper.

'It's coming.' He sounded exasperated. 'You don't want your bacon non-crispy, do you?'

Silence. The sound of spitting bacon.

'If she wasn't here, I'd stay on for a bit,' he said softly. 'But she is. And it's a dangerous road. The twins and you and me…we're a unit and I'm not letting anything threaten that. Or anyone.'

She should go in. The bacon smelled terrific.

She didn't. She went upstairs to check on Angus.

Jake wasn't letting anything threaten his precious family unit, she thought as she trudged upstairs. She didn't intend to let him threaten her independence. Fine. They were of like minds.

All she felt like doing was bursting into tears.

Check Angus. Forget the tears.

Forget men! Or every man but Angus…

She knocked. When Angus didn't answer she opened the door a crack, as she'd been doing since they'd arrived, assuming he was still asleep.

He wasn't asleep. He was sprawled on the floor by the window.

He'd tripped on the mat, she thought in dismay. His oxygen cylinder was on its side and his nasal tube had been ripped from his face in his fall.

No!

'Jake!' she screamed in a voice that was meant to be heard in the middle of next week.

He'd stopped breathing. She couldn't find a pulse. Damn, where was it? She was feeling his carotid artery. His neck was warm to the touch but she couldn't find...she couldn't find...

Airway. Check airways, stupid. Keep the panic for later. Her fingers were in his mouth, seeking for an obstruction and finding none.

Heart attack? Stroke?

Get the breathing back and find out. Get oxygen. A defibrillator?

'Jake!' Angus must be dead if that scream didn't have him jerking to wakefulness.

Don't die, Angus.

Keep yourself professional.

Ha!

She ripped his pyjama coat open, hauling him onto his back. She was kneeling over him, breathing for him, cupping her hands to start the rhythmic pounding of CPR.

How long had he been on the floor? She'd checked him at four a.m. and he'd been fine. How long hadn't he been breathing?

He was still so warm. Maybe...maybe...

From behind her she heard boots taking the stairs three at a time. Then Jake's barked query. 'What the—?'

'It must be cardiac arrest. Have you got—?'

'I'm going.' The boots retreated. Steps retreating, stairs taken four at a time.

She went back to breathing. Went back to pounding. Breathe, then fifteen short, sharp thumps, breathe...

Come on. Come on.

Susie was in the doorway now, leaning heavily on her crutches. How had she got up the stairs? Behind her was Margie, and the twins behind her. Their faces were appalled.

'Keep the littlies away,' she managed between breaths, but every ounce of energy was going into rhythmic pumping.

Jake was back then, pushing them unceremoniously aside, dumping equipment on the floor. A portable defibrillator. Thank God.

Please.

He worked around her, ripping Angus's pyjama jacket further, sticking on patches, readying…

Checking the monitor.

'There's pulse,' he told her. 'There's still pulse.'

'But—'

'It's slow as bedamned. Keep breathing for him, Kirsty.' He was hauling an oxygen mask from his kit. As he readied, Kirsty moved aside. In seconds Jake had the mask fitted and was breathing for him, pushing pure oxygen into Angus's lungs.

Kirsty didn't stop. They needed an IV. Sodium bicarb. Atropine…

What was happening?

Angus had ischaemic heart disease. She knew that. If his pulse hadn't completely gone then maybe this was a mild infarct. Maybe they'd get him back. That was the best-case scenario.

The thought that it could be a stroke with all its ramifications was unbearable.

Her fingers were flying. Jake had the old man's chest moving up and down with a reassuring rhythm. They just had to get him breathing for himself again. Maybe the sodium bicarb. could be enough to prevent any long-term damage.

If he still had a pulse… It must have just happened. Maybe he'd woken with the smell of bacon and the sound of voices in the kitchen. He must have stumbled. As Jake worked to set up an IV line, she was thinking all the time.

Please.

And then a tiny gasp, so small they might have imagined it. But then another. Another and a choking, gasping cough.

Breathing re-established. Breathing re-established!

Dear God.

The old eyes fluttered open. Angus winced as though in pain, and then seemed to focus. On Jake. On to Kirsty.

'Sue...Susie,' he murmured, and Kirsty's eyes flew to the door. But her twin pre-empted her. Susie couldn't have heard Angus's whisper, but sometimes what was said to Kirsty was said to Susie, and Susie was already manoeuvring herself within Angus's field of vision.

'I'm here, Angus.'

He stared up at her, bewildered. Trying to talk. 'Shush,' Jake murmured, but he lifted the mask back so Angus could say what he obviously desperately wanted to say.

'Stay safe,' Angus murmured at last. 'Susie... Rory...'

'I'm safe,' Susie said gently, and she laid her hand on her swollen belly, guessing the core of his fear. 'Rory's baby is safe. We're worried about you.'

'Spike,' he whispered. 'He'll die...'

Kirsty even let herself smile at that. If he was worried about his pumpkin then surely there was hope. Surely there was a tomorrow for this gentle old man who she and her sister were only starting to know.

Who she and her sister were starting to love.

'Susie will take care of your pumpkin,' Jake said softly, and by the look on his face Kirsty knew he was as emotional as she was. 'She won't let him die. Meanwhile, Susie's come a long way to have this baby where you can play great-uncle, so you'd better make an effort for her. You're going to hospital.'

'I'm not.' That was said so loudly, so indignantly that Kirsty wanted to laugh out loud. There were still miracles in this job. Sometimes—just sometimes—she loved being a doctor. To have this outcome...

'Oh, yes, you are, you old coot,' Jake was saying, and there was no disguising the emotion in his voice now. 'You're coming in for complete assessment, and that's an order. Do you really not want to be around to support Susie as she has her baby?'

'I… No.' Kirsty was administering morphine. She could tell he was hurting—badly. Understandably. The way she'd pounded his ribs was enough to make anyone hurt.

'Then you're coming to hospital.'

'Spike,' Angus whispered, and closed his eyes.

'I promise I'll look after your pumpkin,' Susie told him. 'Me and Ben.'

'Come on.' Jake stooped and lifted the old man into his arms, motioning to Kirsty to lift the various pieces of attached medical paraphernalia. 'Kirsty, will you come with me?'

'I can walk,' Angus said weakly.

'Yeah, and I can fly,' Jake retorted. 'But let's not do either unless we have to.'

CHAPTER NINE

Two hours later Kirsty drove back to the castle in a borrowed hospital car, feeling as if maybe, just maybe things would be OK.

The electrocardiogram showed minor damage, as did the cardiac enzymes. Nothing that couldn't repair itself. Angus was sleeping, recovering from the combined effects of painkillers and shock, but his breathing was deep and almost normal.

'He'll go to Sydney and get thorough cardiac assessment now,' Jake growled. 'I haven't been able to get the stubborn old coot into this hospital before this, and I'm going to move so fast he won't know what hit him.' He hesitated. 'Kirsty…'

'You'd like me to go with him?'

His face cleared. 'If you would. I'll take care of Susie for you.'

'Of course you will,' she said softly, and then looked away.

Her job in a hospice at home was often heart-wrenching, but her heart had never been wrenched as it was now. What was it with this place, these people…this man?

She'd fallen in love with a whole community, she thought bleakly as she drove home, and she didn't know what to do about it. Because although she'd fallen for this place, she knew she could never separate the two. Her love for Dolphin Bay and its people.

Her love for Jake.

Maybe a couple of days away would be good for her, she thought. Jake was arranging for air ambulance to transport

Angus that afternoon and the plan was for her to accompany him. As his medical attendant—but also as his family.

Because that's what I am, like it or not, she admitted to herself. Family. Somehow this whole place has wrapped itself around my heart, and I don't know what to do about it.

Do what comes next and nothing more, she told herself fiercely. Go home. Reassure Susie and everyone else. Pack an overnight bag and go to Sydney. Stay there until you're sure Angus is out of danger.

Get away from Jake.

Right.

But when she drove into the castle forecourt there was more drama. She couldn't have time out just yet.

'Spike's dying.'

Kirsty was barely out of the car door before Susie appeared from the gate leading to the kitchen garden. Boris was by her side, looking as concerned as Kirsty.

'Kirsty, Spike's dying,' Susie yelled again. 'Angus must have been trying to tell us…' She was balancing precariously on her crutches. As she saw her twin she took hasty steps forward—too hasty—and started to stagger. Kirsty reached her before she hit the ground.

'Jake phoned,' her sister said. 'He said Angus would be OK and you were going to Sydney. Everyone left and then I came out to see. Kirsty, Spike—'

'Susie, calm down.'

'I'm calm, but—'

'You're not calm. Be sensible. Where's everyone else?'

Susie took a deep breath. She closed her eyes, obviously fighting for composure. 'Ben's gone home to water his own vegetables. Margie says that's the first place he goes when he's upset. Then when Jake phoned and said he wanted you to go to Sydney, Margie said she'd shop now as she doesn't want me to be alone for too long, and after you go I will be. So she and the twins have gone into town. But when they left…' Her voice broke on a sob.

'Hey, hush.' Kirsty put her hand on her twin's, trying to stem what sounded like rising hysteria. 'It's OK.'

'But it's not,' Susie sobbed. 'I know why Angus had his heart attack. He must have seen. When they left I went to check. Angus and I cleared all the leaves near the pumpkin, leaving the stem exposed. Someone's pulled it. They've hauled the roots right out of the ground. I've replanted him, but it'll take days for his roots to re-establish themselves. He's wilting while I watch.'

The pumpkin was indeed poorly. Kirsty's specialty was dying people, not pumpkins—but she knew a dying pumpkin when she saw one. If she'd been selecting pumpkins for a hospice, Spike might well have met her criteria.

He wasn't totally limp. Some of the leaves closer to the roots were still stiff and healthy, but the leaves close to the pumpkin itself were visibly wilting. Susie had rigged up a sheet to give shade. She'd soaked the ground with water, so the patch was sodden, but obviously not enough water was getting through.

'Someone's wrenched him out of the ground,' Susie whispered. 'I guess we were lucky the whole plant didn't break off, but as it is, Spike can't get water and he'll die.'

'Won't it ripen anyway?' Kirsty said doubtfully—and received the look she'd used not so long ago on a junior intern who'd suggested using aspirin for renal colic.

'It's too soon. He'll get bigger before he ripens. If he's picked now he'll never be any good. This must have been why Angus had his attack. He'll have looked out the window and been rushing to help. Who can have done such a thing?' Susie sank onto the wet ground and lifted the main stem into her hands. 'This will break Angus's heart. The damaged roots can't supply enough water to get through.'

Kirsty opened her mouth to say something, and then she stopped.

No. What she was thinking had to be dumb.

'What?' Susie said. 'Why is it dumb?'

'You know, Jake does this to me, too, now,' Kirsty complained. 'Can't a girl even think by herself?'

'Jake loves you as much as I love you,' Susie retorted. 'He just doesn't know it yet. What's dumb?'

Ignore the Jake comment, Kirsty told herself. Concentrate on important matters. Like dying pumpkins.

She was a palliative-care physician. Her specialty was taking care of the dying. Not lifesaving. So far today she'd helped save Angus and now… Could she save a pumpkin? A medical step sideways.

'I was thinking…'

'I know you were thinking,' Susie said, exasperated. 'But you need to stop thinking and do something or the pumpkin's cactus.'

'You know, palliative-care doctors don't use the word cactus,' she said thoughtfully, her mind still racing. 'It's not a good image.'

'Spike will die, then,' Susie said, sounding even more exasperated. And fearful. She'd fallen for Angus in a big way, Kirsty thought. Angus was Rory's uncle and he was therefore Susie's family.

If Angus was Susie's family then Angus was therefore her family. And his pumpkin was heading toward being…cactus.

'Is it just water that's flowing through the stem?' she asked cautiously.

'Yes.'

'Ordinary water?'

'There'll be nutrients as well,' Susie said. 'From the soil. But that's not as important as water.'

Kirsty knelt beside her twin and examined the pumpkin with care. Susie's replanting had worked a little. The leaves closet to the ground were still firm. The wilting leaves were the furthest from the roots, and they were turning more limp by the minute.

'I can't bear it,' Susie moaned. 'How can we tell Angus?'

'Shut up, Suze.' She was examining the stem. It looked tough and prickly. Like a hairy forearm?

'Let's not bury him yet,' she said softly. 'Suze, if you cut off a flower and stick it in a vase it'll suck up water. If you cut this stem and stuck it in water, would it suck it up?'

'The pumpkin will draw water in,' Susie told her. 'But it'd never get enough. And the stem would disintegrate in two or three days, leaving us no better off.'

'But if we could bleed water into the stem...' Kirsty said cautiously. 'Maybe via an IV line. Just until the roots recover.'

There was a moment's silence. 'Oh,' said Susie on a note of discovery. And then, 'Oh-h-h.'

'I'm not sure if it'd work,' Kirsty warned.

'It'd be better than sitting watching him die.'

'And he might get infection from the IV site.'

'There's stuff you put on pruned branches to stop infection.' Susie's despair had suddenly evaporated, transforming into excitement. 'Do you have what you need to put in an intravenous line?'

'Jake's lent me a hospital car. It's the one they take out to emergencies when they need back-up. There's an emergency kit in the back. There has to be an IV kit.'

'Then what are we waiting for?'

'You've done what?' On the end of the line Jake sounded incredulous. He'd rung to tell Kirsty the plane was due to take off at two, and he'd got a step-by-step account of their medical procedure from an excited Susie. But Susie had been too excited to make sense. She'd handed the phone over to Kirsty and gone back outside to continue supervision of their patient.

'We've set up an IV line on Spike,' Kirsty said, trying not to sound smug. 'We used a tiny cannula and we're running straight saline at the rate of 80 mil per hour. The leaves closest to Spike are already starting to stiffen. Believe it or not, it might just work.'

'You're kidding me.'

'You're not the only doctor who can be a generalist when the case requires it,' she told him, giving up on the smug bit. She felt smug. Why not admit it?

'No.' There was a moment's silence. 'Kirsty, do you know how the pumpkin came to be pulled out?'

Kirsty's smugness faded. 'I can't imagine,' she said slowly. 'Maybe...Boris digging?'

'Does it look like Boris has been digging?'

'No.' And suddenly she knew what he was thinking. What she would have thought of if Susie hadn't been so traumatised. Only someone wishing to do enormous ill to Angus would do such a thing.

'Who's there now?' Jake was demanding.

'Me and Susie.'

'Go inside and lock the doors. I'm coming home.'

He was being paranoid, Kirsty thought. OK, Kenneth might well be responsible for an uprooted pumpkin. He'd know how much the pumpkin meant to Angus and it'd be an easy way to hurt him. But as for locking themselves in...

But then she remembered the way Kenneth had looked at Susie and suddenly she stopped thinking Jake was paranoid.

Susie had been inside having a drink when the phone had rung, but she hadn't been able to stay in. She'd returned to the veggie patch, Boris beside her.

Kirsty made her way back there now. Jake was being over-cautious, she told herself. There was no danger.

She rounded the hedge and Kenneth was there. With Susie.

Kenneth was pointing a gun straight at her sister's head.

From heat to icy cold, just like that. The world stilled.

In her nice safe hospice back in nice safe Manhattan Kirsty had an emergency beeper she carried in her pocket, linked to the security service for the main hospital. She'd never used it.

She ached for her beeper right now.

'Kenneth,' she said sharply to distract him, trying to haul that pointing arm away from Susie. Susie was leaning heavily on her crutches, looking ill.

'You're her,' Kenneth said indistinctly, and those two words told Kirsty a lot. They told her that he was ill—his speech was slurred and wary. They told her he was desperate. And they told her that the twin thing was confusing him.

'Who are you?' he demanded.

'I'm Susie,' Kirsty said desperately into the stillness. His finger was around the trigger and she felt sick. 'I'm Rory's wife.'

'No.' He had that right at least. The gun firmed, levelled now at Susie's belly. 'She's the one. She's pregnant. And I've looked it up again. Everything's entailed. The old man dies and the kid gets everything. The title, the land back in Scotland, even most of this place. I'm screwed.' He focused again on Susie. 'I came this morning to make you sorry. I saw the pumpkin and I knew how much the old man loved it and I was right, wasn't I? The shock nearly killed him. They've carted him off with a heart attack and any minute now he'll be dead and what's his will be mine. I've just got to get rid of you.'

'Angus isn't dying,' Kirsty said urgently, but she was ignored.

'I thought when I killed Rory that it'd be easy.'

Dear God. Kirsty saw Susie's face blench and she thought her twin might fall over. She took an involuntary step forward, but the gun waved in her direction and she stilled again.

'That's right,' he snarled. 'You thought it was an accident, didn't you? You all did. It was too damned easy. I knew he was married and I had to move fast. But that place where you lived... All I had to do was fiddle with the steering. You know how easy it is to slice through steering rods? Bash it so it looks like it's been damaged in the past. Cut it almost through and then wait. I hoped you'd both die, but when it was only Rory I didn't care. But I might have known you'd be pregnant.'

'You won't get away with it this time, though,' Kirsty said, trying frantically to keep her voice calm. Controlled. 'You shoot Susie and you'll have a nationwide manhunt starting right now. Kenneth, leave us be. Just go while you can.'

'I'm not shooting you,' he said. 'You think I'm stupid?'

'I think you're pointing a gun at us.'

'And I'll shoot you if I have to,' he told her. 'I'd rather we were all dead than Rory's kid gets the old man's wealth. Rory'd still win that way. But I've set up a better way and you're in it, too, regardless of who the hell you are.'

'You're not going to shoot us?' Anything to keep the attention from Susie, she thought. How long would it take Jake to get there? Too long. She couldn't keep him talking.

'I've fixed it,' he told her, almost triumphant. 'I came here this morning and saw everyone and thought the only way to go was get her…' the gun waved again to Susie '…on her own. Make it seem like an accident. So I rigged the boat and came back.'

'The boat.'

'Down the cliff,' he told her. 'Move.'

'Susie can't climb down the cliff. Susie can barely walk.'

'That's where you come in, then,' he snarled. 'You get her down the cliff or I take her to the steep bit and push her over. Move. Both of you. Now!'

What followed was a nightmare.

The castle was built high above the road. Across the road was the cliff, and a worn track leading down to the beach. Kirsty could scramble down the cliff easily, but for Susie, who'd only just learned to balance herself on her crutches, it was almost impossible.

Almost. If there hadn't been a gun pointing at them it would indeed have been impossible, but he'd given them no choice. Get down to the beach under your own steam or die first.

He was mad enough to do it, Kirsty thought. He had some

slivers of rational thought—one being that it would be better if bodies were found without bullet-holes—but little else. He was having trouble differentiating between Susie and Kirsty. Once he'd met Susie and she'd been like Kirsty. Now Kirsty was like Susie and Susie was different—scarred and pregnant. His muddled mind wasn't too sure, but his crazed logic told him to kill them both.

So the gun pointed at them both. Kirsty struggled to hold her twin upright as they staggered slowly down the path, and she couldn't find a way out.

'Hurry!' Kenneth screamed, but they could go no faster than a snail's pace and even Kenneth had to concede that hurrying was impossible.

Boris loped along beside them, ready for adventure. Kenneth ignored him. The dog was racing back up, over and over again, as if saying, Hurry, hurry, there's a great wet world down here—but Kirsty knew there was no such thing.

Would he kill them on the beach? He had some sort of plan.

How long would Jake take to get home? How long would it take him to know their absence wasn't innocent? He'd know after that barked command to stay inside and lock the doors that she and Susie wouldn't leave, and the cars were testament to that.

But he wouldn't think of the beach. He'd never believe Susie would get that far, and he'd waste valuable time searching the castle, the grounds, the bushland to the rear...

'I can't,' Susie whimpered, and Kirsty's arm came round her, rock solid.

'Yes, you can.'

'Shut up,' Kenneth snapped.

'Kenneth, you're ruining your life, doing this,' she murmured, trying to keep her voice measured, fighting to make him see logic. 'You'll never get away with killing us. Let us go and we'll forget this ever happened.'

'I killed Rory,' he told them, shoving Susie hard with the gun so she fell against Kirsty and Kirsty had to fight to keep her upright. 'You think I'm going to kill my brother and then let some stupid kid take what belongs to me?'

'It belongs to Angus,' she said. One of Susie's crutches had fallen aside. Kirsty was acting as her support on one side and Susie's sole attention was keeping her remaining crutch in place so she wouldn't crumple where she stood. Kirsty was aware that Susie was weeping, but she was weeping silently.

She wasn't fighting, Kirsty thought in despair. It was as if Susie had always known that something like this would happen. Once Rory had died, why go on herself?

She had to fight for them both.

Kenneth's gun jabbed Susie again. 'Faster.'

How could she fight this? Should she drop Susie and launch herself at the gun?

What would James Bond do in a situation like this? she asked herself desperately, and then thought that James Bond didn't have a pregnant, crippled sister to protect as he coped with the bad guy.

If it had just been her...

Even if it had just been her, she had no idea how to escape. How accurate was a gun like that? How fast would she have to run?

James Bond might have all the answers. She had none. All she could do was struggle to hold Susie up and pray.

Jake. Please, Jake.

Finally they reached the beach. They rounded the last rocky outcrop and Kirsty saw that Kenneth had been here before. This must have been what he'd done this morning. He'd come, he'd checked the castle, he'd hauled up his uncle's pumpkin in fury. Then he'd gone away and coldly found what he'd needed.

There were two boats in the cove. A motorboat was anchored a few feet from shore and a dilapidated wooden dinghy was hauled up on the sand. A towrope connected the two.

'Get into the dinghy,' Kenneth snapped. 'Now.'

'What are you going to do?' If it was just her, she could run, she thought desperately. She could take her chances. Dodge or something. Not calmly do as he demanded.

But Susie was immobile, a target who could no more dodge bullets than fly.

'Just shut up and get in.'

They made it to the boat, with Kirsty half pulling Susie, half carrying her. The crutch was useless on the soft sand. Susie was clutching her sister, and Kirsty could feel her shaking.

And suddenly there was a part of Kirsty that stopped being terrified. Suddenly she was just plain angry. Coldly, calculatingly angry.

Would he take them out to sea and shoot them?

'You know, bodies get washed up to shore,' she told him, making her voice flat and emotionless. 'If we're washed up with bullet-holes you'll still be in the frame for murder.'

'You'll not get bullet-holes unless you ask for them,' he snarled. He was standing in the shallows, close to where the motorboat was moored. 'Get into the dinghy.'

Kirsty looked at the scenario and knew what was happening. They'd get in the ancient dinghy, he'd get into the motor boat and he'd tow them out to sea. To what?

Where was Jake? Jake, hurry!

Susie was clutching the side of the dinghy. She fell to her knees and Kirsty dropped onto the sand beside her.

'We have to get in,' she told her. 'Come on. We can both swim. We'll take our chances.'

'He'll kill us.'

'Get in,' Kenneth yelled, and Kirsty started to rise.

'We're working on it.'

Boris was suddenly with them again. He'd been chasing a gull further down the beach but now he came flying along the sand, quivering his delight.

'Get the dog out of it,' Kenneth screamed, and levelled the gun at Boris.

'If you kill the dog it'll still be evidence that you've hurt us,' Kirsty yelled, and the gun lowered.

'Shove him away, then. I don't want him in the boat.'

'Go find Jake, Boris,' Kirsty said—hopelessly. Stupid dog. She needed a Lassie. Lassie would have brought a whole army of rescue personnel by now, and she'd have had Kenneth hand-cuffed to her collar and helpless.

Lassie was away playing movie star. Boris was all she had.

Boris… Lassie…

Her hand fell to the sand. There was a thin strand of dried seaweed lying beside her.

'Go home, Boris,' she said, and she pushed the dog away. Via her neck. Via her collar.

A seagull descended not twenty feet away and Boris was off again, barking wildly as he hared down the beach. The strand of seaweed was dangling from his collar. It stayed put as he ran.

It was all she could do, Kirsty thought bleakly. As a letter for help it lacked a certain *je ne sais quoi* but she had nothing else.

Please, don't let it fall out. Please, let Jake see it.

She could do no more. Two minutes later they were in the dinghy. Kenneth was in the motorboat. He'd towed the dinghy off the sand and they were heading for the open sea.

'Where are they?'

Jake reached the castle just as Margie and the twins returned, and they weren't out of the car before he barked the question. 'Kirsty and Susie. Where are they?'

'They'll be out in the vegetable garden,' Margie said placidly. 'Penelope, you carry the bag with the ice cream. Alice, you're in charge of the meat.'

'Daddy's frightened,' Alice said with perspicacity, but Jake wasn't listening. He was striding through the garden gate, wanting to see for himself.

They weren't in the vegetable garden.

They'd been here, though. He stared at Spike, with his high-tech drip-stand and his IV drip. Despite his unease he felt his lips quirk with amusement. Kirsty was one amazing doctor, he thought. He looked at the neat bandage wrapping the needle to Spike's stem and thought, Wow.

She was no palliative-care physician. She brought patients back from the dead.

They'd be inside. They must be.

They weren't.

'No one's home, Daddy,' Penelope told him as he burst through the kitchen door. 'We went to see if Susie wanted ice cream. Aren't they in the garden?'

'Are you worried about Kenneth?' Margie asked, her eyes clouding as she caught his fear. She was speaking lightly so as not to concern the girls, but Jake's daughters were bright.

'Is the nasty man here again?' Alice asked.

'I don't think so,' Jake said, but his hand was already reaching for his phone. He wanted the police. He wanted help. Now!

'Here's Boris,' Alice said as Boris raced through the open back door. 'Yuck. He's all wet.'

'And he's got stuff stuck in his collar,' Penelope said. 'Seaweed.'

Kenneth was crazy, but not stupid.

Once they were in the boat Kirsty had had a vague idea that they could jump out and swim. The day was hot and calm, and even if Susie couldn't swim far, she could float. If he simply dumped them at sea then they had a chance. But Kenneth had never intended that they simply be dumped. He was crazy but there still seemed logic in his plan.

He kept his gun trained on Susie. She was the one who couldn't move with speed, and he must have known instinctively that Kirsty would never leave her. He trained the gun on them until their boat was wrenched off the beach and the motorboat hit full throttle. Kirsty's small hope died. The water was so still that even if they jumped, all he had to do was take pot shots at them until they were dead.

Maybe he knew where there were sharks, Kirsty thought, and the idea made her even colder, made her heart almost stop.

The old wooden boat was hardly seaworthy. It was taking in water but that was the least of her terrors. Susie was crouched in the bow and Kirsty had her arms around her, taking comfort as much as giving it.

'What'll he do?'

'I don't know,' Kirsty said.

And then she glanced ahead and suddenly she did know.

They were a mile—maybe two—offshore. Here the smoothness of the sea was broken by a line of ragged rocks, seemingly emerging from the ocean floor. Eight or so rocks. A tiny reef. Like a row of vicious teeth, with a couple broken off.

Kenneth was heading straight towards it, faster and faster. He'd put his gun down, and in the full sunlight Kirsty saw the flash of a knife.

She knew what he intended.

He'd take them in so they were headed straight for the rocks and then he'd slice the towrope, Kirsty thought in horror. They'd continue so fast that their boat would splinter on the reef. And afterwards...

She never got to afterwards. She was hauling Susie away from the bow of the boat, screaming to her, hauling her to the side, to the lowest point.

'He's going to smash us on the rocks,' she screamed. Dear God...

If they jumped now they'd still be in calm water, she thought. He'd still be able to get near them. Their only hope was in waiting.

And Susie knew. Her twin's hand held hers, steadying. When one twin was in danger, the other knew, and how much more so now when they were both in deadly peril.

Kenneth had turned away, watching the reef. He had to. He

needed to steer until he was almost on the rocks, waiting until the last possible moment so they had maximum velocity...

Wait.

She didn't have to say it. They'd hauled themselves hard up on the side of the boat and for a sickening moment the boat lurched and Kirsty thought it might go over.

Too soon. Too soon.

Kenneth's boat was a hundred yards from the reef. Fifty. Thirty. Now!

It happened so fast. The cable was sliced through, the boat lurched with their sideways motion, but kept going, kept going...and the women inside fell backwards out of the boat and slammed hard against the surface of the water.

CHAPTER TEN

THE impact stunned Kirsty. There was a sharp, hot pain across her chest that threatened to overwhelm her as she sank. But Susie's hand was in hers. Susie was still with her and as she rose to the surface she felt Susie's grip tighten.

They'd waited almost too long. Almost. The boat's momentum had become their momentum, so they were in the wash of white water around the rocks. And there was a spray of wood around them. Splintering parts of the dinghy that had gone forward and smashed hard into the rocks. Without them.

They were safe?

Not yet.

Kenneth would still be concentrating on getting his boat clear, Kirsty thought in the vestige of brain she had left to think of things apart from breathing and staying afloat and ignoring the pain in her chest. He'd come so close that he'd have had to pull an almost one-eighty-degree turn to haul his boat away.

Susie was tugging her. Injured and pregnant as she was, Susie was rising to their need faster than Kirsty.

The waves were crashing against the rocks. This could be a maelstrom at times, but not today. Today the sea was kind. The waves weren't so great they couldn't fight them, and Susie's hand was hauling her further into the white water rather than away from it.

In the white water lay their only protection. Kenneth mustn't see them. Both of them knew that.

Their hope lay in him being too intent on hauling his boat away from the rocks to have seen what they'd done.

So they surfaced but they surfaced with fear. With their heads barely above the water, Susie made a tiny hand movement, a movement like that of a porpoise.

Maybe he'd picked the wrong twins for a watery death, Kirsty thought, fighting back pain, and for a moment she allowed herself a glimmer of hope. She and Susie had played water polo—had lived for the game as youngsters. Susie's hand movement meant *Meet you under water in that direction.*

A fast glance showed she was indicating the only gap in the line of rocks. The gap held a mass of white water but maybe it was possible. And if they could get through…

They couldn't do it with linked hands and both of them knew it. Susie's legs were so weak she'd be slow, but the pain in Kirsty's chest meant that she'd be limited as well. She'd cracked a rib, she thought, and gave herself a tiny test. Breathe in. Breathe out. It hurt but her breathing wasn't impeded.

Maybe she hadn't punctured a lung.

Susie's hand was squeezing hers and her eyes were questioning. She'd know Kirsty was in pain.

But they had no choice and both of them knew it.

Meet you through the rocks?

Go. Now.

And amazingly she did it. Kirsty used her feet, kicking hard under the surface of the water, duck-diving, ignoring the scream of protest in her chest.

Somehow she found the gap. The waves were crashing against her, pushing her sideways. She had to surface just for a moment to reorientate, to breathe, but the gap was right where she'd seen it and down she went again—and through.

Through.

She surfaced.

And then she had to wait. Only for seconds, but they stayed as some of the longest seconds in her life. Please, let Susie be safe. How could she get through? Her legs had no strength. She was eight months pregnant. Eight months pregnant! Please…

And then the water exploded beside her and her twin was with her, and she was even laughing!

This was the Susie who'd been at her side since childhood, a tomboy, a reckless, brave, laughing hothead who'd chosen landscape gardening as a profession because she'd loved playing in mud, and whose light had only been dimmed by Rory's death. Somehow in the past few days the old Susie had started to resurface, and now Kenneth's threats had lifted her right back to life.

'Let him get us now,' Susie said. She grabbed Kirsty's hands and they were treading water behind the rocks. Their heads were still barely above the water and there were waves breaking between them and the horizon. Even if Kenneth brought the boat round to their side of the rocks, he wouldn't be able see them. The only way he could was to bring his boat so far that he'd risk his own boat being smashed.

How long should they stay there?

How long would Kenneth wait? He'd see that their boat was a splintered mess. He would assume that they'd be injured at the very least, desperately injured and miles from the mainland.

He wouldn't wait long, Kirsty thought, and they could stay treading water.

'What's hurting?' Susie asked.

'I think I might have cracked a rib,' Kirsty told her. 'No drama. How about you?'

'I can tread water for hours.'

No, she couldn't, Kirsty thought. She wasn't as strong as she'd thought. The adrenalin was high now, but after an hour or so in the water…

Maybe they could get up onto one of the rocks. In a little while she'd check and see if it was possible.

But not yet. Not yet.

Jake, you have to find us.

The beach was deserted, but there were signs that there'd been people there. There were footsteps in the sand. Three different ones. Two smaller—women's. One larger. And a dog's pawprints.

There was a deep indentation in the sand. A boat had been dragged up here and then dragged off again.

He had them in a boat, Jake thought, his heart almost stopping. Where...?

'We'll call in the chopper.' Fred Mackie, Dolphin Bay's only policeman, was looking as grim as Jake felt. 'If it's not being used, they can get here in less than half an hour.'

'Half an hour.'

Fred's hand was on Jake's shoulder. 'Meanwhile I'll have every boat out of harbour searching.'

'If he kills them at sea...'

'He's mad but not that mad,' Fred said, uneasily, though, since Fred had known Kenneth as a boy. 'I'll call in the psychiatric crisis assessment team.'

The phone sounded on Jake's belt. If he'd been sensible, Jake wouldn't have answered it, but he answered automatically.

'Jake?'

It was Angus. What the hell?

'They're saying he has the girls.' Angus sounded breathless and desperately worried.

'Now, don't—'

'Don't protect me,' Angus snapped. 'The nurses here have been doing that. I knew something was wrong. Word travels round this place faster than you'd believe, and the girl who came to take my obs looked sick. Wouldn't tell me why and that made me think it had to be Kenneth. So I rang Ben Boyce and he's with me now.'

'Don't worry—'

'Of course I'm worrying,' he snarled. 'I should have found the strength to say something this morning. I saw Spike and I knew it had to be him. The thing is…I know where he might have taken them.'

'Where?'

'He's dead scared of guns,' Angus said. 'Fascinated by them but when they go off he turns to jelly. His father used to tease him with them, which helped a whole lot, I don't think. I'm telling you now that he might threaten them with a gun but I doubt he'd use it. But if he wanted to do mischief…'

'Tell me.'

'There's Rot-Tooth Rocks,' Angus said, and Jake thought he should stop him now because he could hear from Angus's whispered speech that the old man was pushing himself past the limit to impart what he felt he ought to. 'A line of rocks about two miles out to sea. Nor-nor east. You look on a nautical map…'

'I'll find them,' Jake said quickly. 'Why do you think they're there?'

'Kenneth killed a dog that way once,' Angus whispered. 'Rory's dog. That was why Rory left. Rory was staying with me—him and his great black Lab that went everywhere with him. Kenneth came down and hated Rory being here. He took the Lab out to sea on a makeshift raft and dashed him against the rocks.'

'Oh, God.'

'Move fast, Jake,' Angus whispered. 'Move fast.'

They had to get out of the water.

They'd crouched behind the rocks for fifteen minutes now, growing colder and more terrified by the minute. Kirsty's chest was hurting but that was the least of her worries. Susie was growing quieter. Finally she stopped talking altogether; she stopped responding to Kirsty's prompts. Kirsty thought,

Enough. It was a risk to leave their safe haven but a bigger risk to stay.

One of the rocks had a flattish surface, just clear of the water. If they could manage...

'Susie, I'm climbing up. I'll tug you up after me.'

Susie didn't answer.

Kirsty hauled her round to face her. Susie's eyes were wide with pain, focused inward.

'What's wrong?'

'Nothing.'

Yeah, right. But she had no choice.

At least the tide was going out. More of the rocks were being exposed, meaning once they got onto the rock they'd be out of the water for hours.

Long enough for Jake to find them?

As long as Kenneth had gone.

Please...

She grabbed Susie's hands and tugged her across the gap to the flat rock. If they had both been well, this would have been a cinch, but Susie's legs were so weak, and she was so bulky and Kirsty's chest hurt...

She paused and did a bit more test breathing. If it hurt this much she surely must have punctured a lung—but her breathing was OK.

'I'm being a wuss,' she whispered to Susie and Susie managed a reply.

'Twin wusses. Wusses who have to climb a rock.'

And somehow they did. Kirsty first, waiting for a wave to give her momentum, hauling herself up, trying not to cry out as her chest hit the flat, unforgiving surface. Trying not to stay flailing like a beached whale, trying to look up, searching the horizon, fearful that Kenneth would be just...there.

The horizon was empty.

Problem number one despatched, she thought with a

twinge of triumph before the bigger twinge of her cracked rib washed back.

Ignore the rib. Now Susie.

And she did have to ignore the rib. The only way to get Susie onto the rock was to reach down with both hands and pull.

Where was her doctor's bag when she needed it? Her kingdom for morphine.

Morphine wasn't available. Forget morphine. She pulled and Susie tried to help and couldn't. Twice Kirsty hauled and she didn't think she could do it, but then a wave, bigger than the rest, washed in and lifted Susie's body momentarily. She slithered onto the rock so there were two beached whales now.

They lay, unmoving, not speaking, while Kirsty's pain subsided from agony to just plain awful.

But they'd done it. They were out of the water and Kenneth was gone.

Jake would come.

'We're OK,' she whispered, and reached out to squeeze Susie's hand.

Susie squeezed back with such force that Kirsty yelped.

'We now only have one problem,' Susie whispered at last.

'Which is?' Kirsty wasn't so sure about not having punctured her lung now. She found she could scarcely breathe.

'I think I've just had my fourth contraction.'

'How fast can we make this thing go?'

Rod Hendry's fishing trawler was the only boat in harbour that was complete with skipper when Jake and Sgt Mackie arrived to commandeer anything that moved. The policeman was now barking orders into his radio while Jake stood by Rod at the tiller and pushed him to go faster.

'If we go any faster, mate, the engine will go ahead without the boat,' Rod told him. 'I'm doing faster'n safe as it is.' Then his eyes narrowed against the sun. 'Speaking of fast...who the hell is that?'

Jake looked. He grabbed Rod's field glasses and focused. A speedboat. Powerful. A man crouched low in the back.

'That'd be Scott Curry's speedboat,' Rod said. 'I saw it go out earlier.' He frowned. 'That can't be right. Scott's in Queensland.'

'It'll be Kenneth,' Jake said flatly. The speedboat was altering course now, moving away from the fishing boat rather than closer to it. 'Fred!' he yelled to the policeman, and Fred gazed through the glasses as Jake explained.

'You want me to chase him?' Rod asked, semi-hopeful, but they all knew chasing a speedboat with a fishing trawler was impossible.

'I'll contact base,' Fred said grimly. 'He's alone in the boat now. I'll have someone else pick him up. Meanwhile…'

'We get to the rocks,' Jake demanded. 'Go!'

'If he was towing a dinghy with a boat that powerful…' Fred said thoughtfully, but Jake cut him off before he could finish. They all knew what could have happened. What had probably already happened.

'I said I wouldn't date her,' Jake whispered, and Fred looked at his family's doctor in surprise.

'That'd be a first,' he said, gently teasing. 'You wanting to date someone.'

'I don't want to date her,' Jake said desperately. 'I want to marry her.'

'Two-inch dilatation. Susie, you're moving like a train. You have to slow down.'

'How can I slow down?' Susie whispered desperately. 'Cross my legs? I don't think so. Ow!'

'Pant through contractions,' Kirsty told her. 'Whatever you do, don't push.'

First labours were supposed to be long, she thought desperately. But, then, Susie had already gone into premature labour once and it had been suppressed.

There was nothing here to suppress labour. She needed alcohol drips, sedation, quiet.

And if the baby was born...

They were wet and cold already. They had nothing to warm a premature baby.

It would hardly be prem. Susie was only three weeks before full term.

It couldn't come.

She hauled her soaking windcheater over her head and folded it so Susie had something approaching a pillow. Their rock was all of five feet long by three feet wide. It sloped, two feet above the water at one end, one foot at the other.

As a delivery room, it made a great rock.

'I'm scared,' Susie whimpered, and Kirsty hauled herself together and tried to sound professional.

'Now, now, Mrs Douglas, what on earth is there to fret about? Women have babies all the time. This is just a water birth with a difference.'

Susie tried to smile—but failed. 'I want my bath heated, please, Doctor.'

'Nonsense.' She had to pause as another contraction washed over her twin. Less than two minutes apart. Uh-oh. Susie was gripping her hand so tightly she was almost reaching bone. 'You'll write a book about this,' she told Susie as the pain eased. 'Natural birth with a difference. Sea, sun and dolphins, and no intervention at all.'

'I'd like Enya on the stereo,' Susie said, trying to match her mood.

'No Enya.' Kirsty was clutching at straws. 'We'd need technology to play Enya, and think of the germs we'd have to contend with. Hospitals are full of golden staph, and I bet sound systems have their share, too. You wouldn't want your baby catching golden staph.'

'No, indeed.' Susie took a rasping breath and humour died. 'Kirsty, I can't really have my baby on this rock.'

'I suspect you don't have a choice,' Kirsty said, and as the next contraction hit she thought, no, it was more than a suspicion.

They were miles from anywhere. When the tide came in they'd be in the water. Somewhere there was Kenneth, intent on murder.

And they were having a baby.

'If I ever suggested I didn't need a man in my life, can I change my mind now?' she said under her breath. 'Jake, I need you. Now!'

'Rot-Tooth Rocks are that white line on the horizon.'

The moment Rod said it, Jake had the field glasses fixed on the horizon. 'Can't we go faster?'

He was ignored.

Closer.

'I think…' Jake was straining to see and Rod grabbed the glasses back from him. The big fisherman's eyes were creased from staring at the sea all his life. He focused. And what he saw…

He dropped the glasses and gunned the motor so hard black smoke started coming out the rear.

'Hey,' the police sergeant said, startled. 'You'll kill us.'

'They're on the rock,' Rod snapped. 'From here…one's crouching over but one…hell, maybe one's dead.'

'There's a boat coming.' Kirsty whispered it to Susie but Susie was no longer listening. She was in a mist of pain and terror. She should have an epidural, Kirsty thought numbly. To have this type of pressure on her already damaged back… To have this level of pain…

There was a boat coming.

Was it Kenneth? It was still too far away to make out.

They couldn't slip back down into the water now. They couldn't hide.

Another contraction, merging into the last.

'No,' Susie screamed. 'Kirsty, no…'

'Breathe into it,' Kirsty said, firmly releasing the clutching fingers and moving to where she needed to be. Which gave her exactly six inches of balancing space before she toppled into the sea. 'OK, Susie, if you must, you must. Push.'

'Kirsty!'

They were near enough to be heard. Jake was at the side of the boat, yelling frantically to the girls on the rock.

Kirsty was kneeling over Susie and he couldn't see...he couldn't see...

She must be able to hear him.

'Kirsty!'

Fifty yards. Thirty.

'I daren't go closer,' Rod muttered, but before he finished saying it Jake was over the side, stroking his way desperately through the white water.

One minute Kirsty was frantic. Despairing. The next Jake was beside her, hauling himself up on the rock. Assessing fast.

'What's happening?' he snapped, and Kirsty gave a choked cry of fear and shock.

Jake was grasping her shoulders, pulling her aside. She was too close to Susie for him to be able to see.

'Back into medical mode here, Dr McMahon.'

And, snap, just like that, it returned. Somehow. Enough for her to be able to falter, 'The cord. It's round the neck. I can't stop...'

She was picked up and lifted to the other end of the rock where there was a tiny amount of space by Susie's head. Jake was crouching down, his big hands moving.

'Susie, stop pushing,' he snapped, so loudly that Kirsty jumped in shock.

'Pant. Don't push. You're not to push, Susie. Stop!'

Kirsty knew what he was doing. It was what she'd been trying to do but her hands were so cold they were numb, the pain in her chest was too sharp, she didn't have the strength...

He'd be pushing the baby back. Just a bit. Just a little so he could manoeuvre…

'There.' It was a sigh of triumph, and Susie cried out.

'I can't—I can't…'

'It's OK,' Jake said, still triumphant. 'Push, Susie, love. Go for it.'

And ten seconds later Rosie Kirsteen Douglas emerged into the world. Two miles out to sea, on a flat piece of rock not much bigger than a man. Seven pounds eleven ounces, and with the healthiest set of lungs a baby could be blessed with.

Jake held her in his hands, moving swiftly, ripping up his shirt, tying the cord with a scrap of fabric, holding her up—just for a second—so the men in the boat could see, holding her for another millisecond so Kirsty could see, and then smiling down at Susie, showing her her baby and tucking the tiny newborn under Susie's sodden windcheater, tight against her skin.

After the mammoth effort Susie had made, her breasts had to be warmest place available, Kirsty thought. It was the warmest place until they could get themselves off the rock.

Sensible.

But Kirsty was no longer sensible. Susie was smiling and smiling, cradling her body into a protective curve, no longer aware of anything but this new little life that was gloriously hers.

Kirsty was weeping. Her head was in her hands and she was out of control, and when Jake swore and managed to get himself to where he could reach her, touch her, take her into his arms and hold her, the weeping only grew worse.

She was lost.

She didn't cry. She never cried.

She cried now as if she'd cry for ever.

CHAPTER ELEVEN

SHE woke and she was on the wrong side of a hospital bed. The inside rather than the outside. It was so extraordinary that she had to shake her head to make herself believe she wasn't dreaming.

Shaking her head wasn't a good idea. Shaking anything wasn't good.

She stayed very still indeed, and when Babs tiptoed in to do her obs and Kirsty spoke, Babs gave a squeak of surprise.

'I thought you were asleep.'

'Just very, very still,' Kirsty said cautiously. She reached out and grabbed Babs's wrist, anxious that this contact with the outside world not be broken. 'What's happening?'

'You're black and blue and red all over,' Babs said cheerfully. 'If you want a more technical medical diagnosis, I'll have to get your doctor. Which, since your doctor has been pacing the corridor for the past two hours waiting for you to wake up, won't be too hard at all. Let me take your blood pressure and temp. and I'll fetch him.' And then, as she looked at Kirsty's face, she grinned and relented. 'OK, I'll fetch him now. Something tells me your blood pressure before and after you see your treating doctor might be very different.'

Before Kirsty could reply, she'd whisked herself out of the room—and one minute later Jake was there. He stood in the doorway with such an expression of anxiety on his face that Kirsty almost laughed. Almost. You had to move your chest to laugh and she wasn't about to do any such thing.

'Jake.'

In two strides he'd reached her, taking her hand, stooping to kiss her forehead, her lips.

'Kirsty…'

'Hey, am I dying?' she managed weakly. 'I don't even act like this with patients two minutes before the end.'

'You could have died,' he growled, his voice breaking with emotion. He hauled a chair up and sat beside her, without letting go of her hand. Which was very satisfactory indeed. 'Kirsty, will you marry me?'

Her world stilled. Marry…

Too much was happening too fast. This was crazy. It couldn't be happening.

'Um, no,' she whispered, and then at the look on his face she added an addendum. 'Well, not yet. There's things I need to sort out first.'

His face cleared. 'I haven't actually got the marriage celebrant out in the hall,' he told her with a rueful smile—and kissed her again. 'What do we need to sort out?'

She was having trouble sorting out her head.

'I've been asleep?'

'We gave you ten milligrams of morphine before we winched you off the rock,' he told her.

'You gave me morphine?'

'I was so worried about the baby I didn't see you were in trouble,' he said. 'Then you disintegrated…'

Hey! 'I did not disintegrate.'

'There's my girl,' he said approvingly. 'OK, you had a wee sniffle. You sniffled until the medical evacuation helicopter arrived from Barnham. We winched Susie and the little one up and lowered them onto the boat. Then we put the harness on you and you proceeded to pass out.'

'I'm sure I didn't,' she said with an attempt at indignation, which didn't quite come off.

'There's no shame in passing out when some stupid medic tries to winch a patient with two broken ribs,' he told her. 'Rule at accident scenes: examine and don't take anyone's word that they're not injured. Hell, Kirsty, your chest is a mess. You must have thumped into a rock when you went overboard. Susie said you hauled her up onto the rock, and how you did it…' His voice broke. 'I've heard of mothers lifting cars off injured kids. Adrenalin or something. It was the bravest—'

'Susie,' she said, cutting across a description that was starting to unsettle her more even than she was already unsettled. It wasn't so much what he was saying, it was how he was looking at her as he said it. Like he'd found a new world. 'Tell me about Susie,' she managed before he could start again, and he took a couple of seconds to recover his voice, to make it work again.

'Susie's great. We winched her and the baby over to the boat but she proceeded to sit up and watch as you were winched off. The moment she realised you'd passed out it was like she'd assumed another body. She was battered and bruised and she'd just given birth. After the battering she'd taken she should have been unconscious herself. Instead, she was hugging her baby so tight it took two of us to prise her away so we could examine her. She was sitting up on the deck, yelling at us to take care of you and to bring more doctors. She was saying that I was too emotionally involved to treat you, and she wanted specialists, and to get a team of the best doctors down at the wharf to take control the moment we docked….'

Kirsty smiled. That was the Susie she knew. Bossy. Happy. In charge of her world.

Oh, welcome back, Susie.

'And the baby really is fine?'

Jake smiled, a lovely, wide smile that encompassed the world. 'Rose is gorgeous. Rose and her mother are currently asleep in the ward next door. In the next bed is Angus, who's refused to go to Sydney until he's seen you safe. He and Susie have both gone to sleep with Rosie's incubator between them, and I can't tell who looks the proudest.'

'Incubator?'

'Only until we're absolutely sure she's warm. But it's a precaution I'm sure we don't need. She's fine.'

'How wonderful.'

But there was one more question. One more thing that had to be asked. 'Kenneth?'

His face clouded. 'Can it wait?'

'No.'

His hold on her hand tightened. 'Not good.'

'Tell me.'

'We saw him while we were heading out to the rocks,' Jake said softly. 'Angus told us where to look—and why. What he said made us think we ought to keep on going. But the police sergeant got on the radio and by the time Kenneth reached harbour he had a reception committee.'

'But they didn't arrest him?' There was something about his voice that told her...

'He headed out to sea again. The fisheries and wildlife patrol boat went after him. They followed him for about half an hour, not approaching, just waiting for him to run out of fuel. They knew he was sick.'

'Then?' Kirsty asked, but by the look on Jake's face she already knew what was coming.

'He came close to shore,' Jake said grimly. 'They thought he'd beach the boat and make a run for it. Then, at the last minute, he just hit the throttle, took the boat up to maximum speed—which on that boat is enormous—and steered straight at the rocks. He didn't stand a chance.'

Oh, no. She lay still, letting the enormity of what had happened sink in. 'Dear God.'

'Mental illness is such a void,' Jake said sadly. 'There's so much we don't know. Maybe if I had my time again I'd train to be a psychiatrist.'

'And then Dolphin Bay would miss out on having the best family doctor in the world,' Kirsty said softly. 'Oh, Jake…'

'Which leads back to my original question,' Jake whispered. 'I've just watched a doctor under the most extraordinarily difficult circumstances rescue a patient from drowning, perform a flawless delivery—'

'Hey, you delivered—'

'Perform a flawless delivery,' Jake repeated. 'Knowing to a nicety when to accept help—'

'It was *your* timing—'

But he wasn't letting her get a word in edgeways. 'And you did all that when you were so battered yourself that you should have been prostrate with pain. I've decided this place needs another doctor. I decided that a long time ago but now I'm certain. And that other doctor's you, Kirsty McMahon. I love you so much…'

'You can't love me.'

'How can I not?'

'You don't do love any more.'

'Yes, I do. Now I do.'

'I propositioned you,' she whispered. 'I goaded you on.'

'And very nicely you goaded, too. But you only asked for a kiss.' He assumed a look of virtue. 'I'm taking it further. I'm asking for your hand in marriage.'

It was too much. The pain was whirling back again, making her senses swim. She looked up into his eyes and she saw love and desire, and all she wanted to do was sink into those eyes…forget…forget…

Marriage.

Jake.

'This isn't fair,' Jake whispered, seeing the doubt and confusion and pain in her eyes. 'I won't push you.'

'I can't think.' She had to think. She must. Jake…

'Don't,' he said softly. He bent and kissed her lightly on the forehead, brushing the salt-stiff curls away and letting his fingers rest on her face. 'I'll give you something now that'll send you right back into the land of nod, and when you wake up we can start again.'

'Start...'

'Let's start again. Kirsty,' he said softly. 'Let's forget you propositioned me. Let's forget I was a dope, and now let's forget I proposed marriage. But also...let's forget your fear of commitment, your belief that the people around you will die, your fear of moving forward. Sleep, my lovely Kirsty, and wake up to your new world. Our new world. Starting now.'

He kept to his word.

For the next few weeks, while Kirsty's battered body healed, while she came to terms with what had happened and while her world righted itself on its axis, Jake left talk of marriage alone.

Firstly he was her doctor. One of the fractured ribs was displaced, with sharp rib ends protruding toward the lung, and when the air ambulance took Angus to Sydney it took Kirsty as well. She needed specialist thoracic surgery. 'You were so lucky you didn't pierce a lung,' Jake growled when he showed her the X-rays. The fragmented bone was so close. So close...

He strapped her with professional care, he handed her over to the care-flight doctors with clinical efficiency, and only at the last minute did he stoop and kiss her, hard, briefly, lovingly, on the lips.

He didn't ring her in Sydney more than a concerned family doctor might have. A very caring doctor...

She'd spent a week in Sydney. A kindly anaesthetist had given her an intercostal block. Out of pain, she'd slept and slept, and her doctors had looked at the amount she'd been sleeping and decreed that she take as long as she needed.

So when she returned—by road ambulance this time—Angus was ready to return with her. His bypass had been gloriously successful. He still had his pet-dog-oxygen-cannister with him, but his breathing was easy, his eyes were alive with excitement and he beamed all the way home.

He had Susie to go home to.

For Susie would stay as long as the old man had left, Kirsty thought. Susie had rung her over and over while she'd been in Sydney. She had described the perfection of her daughter. She had described how much better her walking was without the burden of pregnancy. And Kirsty was no sooner back at the castle than she was taken out to be shown Spike.

'Jake's been replenishing his IV drip every day,' Susie told her. 'He's been wonderful.'

'Is he still staying here?'

'He took the girls home this morning,' Susie said—with no more than a sideways glance at her sister. 'He said you and Angus needed to rest and you'll rest better without the twins and Boris around all the time. Margie has arranged for her sister to help with the housework until we're all fit again.'

Which would be soon, Kirsty thought, watching her sister cradling her baby daughter, watching her laugh with Angus, boss Angus, boss Kirsty into resting… She'd dreaded the baby's birth, fearing postnatal depression. Instead, the birth had catapulted Susie to the other side.

'So Jake will come…when?'

'He said he'll come tonight and every night while we still need him,' Susie told him. 'For Angus.'

For Angus.

And it was for Angus. Jake arrived that night and he spent half an hour with the earl. He came downstairs and chatted to Kirsty and Susie, and if his eyes were warm and loving as they looked at Kirsty…well, they were warm when they looked at Susie as well, and also as he looked down into Rosie's cradle and smiled and gave the tiny baby his little finger to hold.

Kirsty walked him to the door afterwards and tried to thank

him, but he took her shoulders in his hands and kissed her—lightly on the lips but still far too lightly for her liking—and put her away again.

'Don't thank me for loving, Kirsty,' he told her. 'It's all coming together.'

For both of them. She knew it. But it was as if they both needed time now, space to come to terms with what they knew was inevitable. She knew the townsfolk were looking at them, but she didn't mind. She knew Susie was big with questions but she didn't mind that either.

One day soon it'd be right but not yet...not yet.

Her job back home was still waiting for her. She made no irrevocable decision, but she did phone Robert and tell him that he should find someone else.

'It's a shame,' Robert said. 'We've always been such good friends.'

Yes, but I've found more, she thought, but she didn't say it. She hardly dared say it herself.

She didn't think of the future.

As her ribs healed she did a little medicine—she ran a few clinics, she went out to see Mavis and spent quite some time at that lady's bedside.

Like Susie, Mavis wasn't asking questions. She was almost totally pain-free now, and her bright, inquisitive mind was working at full capacity—but she made no comment about Kirsty and Jake.

It was time out. It was a time of knowing that happy ever after was just around the corner but not to be rushed...not to be rushed...

And then came Harvest Thanksgiving.

Harvest Thanksgiving in Dolphin Bay was huge. From the moment Kirsty had entered the town she'd known that this was the biggest festival on the calendar. It took the form of a fête, a two-day celebration where fun and laughter and affirmation of life was the order of the day.

It was also Spike's moment of glory.

The district's best jams and jellies, most obedient dog, highest sponge—and widest pumpkin—were all on show.

Angus was to open the proceedings.

He fretted for days beforehand. 'I couldn't be doing it last year,' he told them. 'I had pneumonia. But I'll be getting there this year if it kills me.'

It almost did. He spent two hours getting into his full Scottish regalia and at the end he had to have a wee lie down. Kirsty went into his bedroom and found him gasping without oxygen.

'If you think you can open the festival dead, you can think again,' she told him, hooking up his oxygen tube and swiping his hand away as he tried to protest.

'The Laird of Loganaich would never have anything as sissy as an oxygen cylinder,' he told her, and Kirsty gazed around the room, saw a discarded sash and wound the offending cylinder with the Douglas clan.

'There,' she said. 'The Laird of Loganaich would find it impossible to leave his loyal and appropriately clad companion behind.'

'You'd be as bossy as your sister.'

'No one's as bossy as Susie.'

'Susie's staying on,' Angus said in quiet satisfaction. 'She's promised. How about you, lass?'

Kirsty fiddled, adjusting the tartan.

'You're marking time,' Angus said softly. 'Waiting for what?'

'To be sure,' she whispered.

'He's sure.'

He was. Every day Kirsty saw Jake's certainty grow. He still didn't push her. He was simply her friend—the friend who laughed with her, who talked to her of her patients as she grew more enmeshed in this little community, who shared the love and laughter of his little girls...

'You can't be keeping him waiting for ever,' Angus said, and Kirsty nodded, tying the sash with a defiant tug.

'I know.'

'So what's holding you back?'

'It's like…I've been so self-contained for so long,' she whispered. 'But now I'm happy.'

'You'd be fearful that if you take the next step you'll compromise what you already have?'

'My mother's death tore my family apart,' she told him. 'My parents were in love, but after Mom died, Dad just…stopped. And Susie—she gave herself completely, and when Rory died she came close to dying as well.'

'So you'll not go that last step.'

'I…I will.' She knew she must. She loved Jake so much. But this last step…

'It's a hard hurdle,' Angus told her, between deep breaths that replenished his oxygen-starved lungs. 'But it's part of life, lass. You love and risk losing, or you don't love at all and then you've lost already. Deirdre and I had the best fun. Here I am left with just a bunch of plastic chandeliers and old Queen Vic in the bathroom—but I wouldn't be having it any other way. I had forty glorious years of my lovely Deirdre, and here I am falling in love all over again with a wee mite called Rose who's twisted around my heart like…'

He paused as the sound of a horn sounded from the forecourt and wiped a surreptitious tear from his wrinkled cheek. 'Enough. I'll be getting maudlin. But don't you be risking things by waiting too long, lass.'

No. She wouldn't.

All she had to do was say yes, she thought as she drove her cargo of Angus and Susie and Rosie in her baby seat—and Spike in a trailer in the rear—to the fair.

Jake was already there. Alice and Penelope whooped up to them the minute they arrived, big with all the news of girls who'd been deprived of their favourite people for a whole two days.

They talked, Jake chatted and joked with Angus and Susie, but all the time Kirsty knew Jake was watching her.

No, she thought. It was different. He wasn't watching her. He was just…with her.

She had to take this leap. She loved him. All she had to do was say yes.

But she stood apart a little. Part of this extended family but not quite taking this final step. Not quite.

Angus played his part in style. That choked her up. The bagpipes started, reaching a crescendo of drums and music that could have come straight from a grey Scottish gloaming. And then there was Angus's speech, full of wry humour, pulling in each and every one of the people present.

He truly was the laird, Kirsty thought, her eyes misting with love for the old man. His speech was hardly marred by his need for oxygen and the cylinder was inconspicuous behind him.

How long did he have?

Pulmonary fibrosis was a killer. Soon…soon.

Not now. She glanced up and Jake's eyes were on her. She met his look full on.

Soon.

The pumpkin judging was early on the agenda. At the appointed hour Kirsty and Jake brought the trailer round and hauled in a few hands to help tug Spike onto the judging dais.

There were yells of appreciation.

'He has to win,' Kirsty said.

'Thanks to Dr McMahon and her magic medication,' Jake said, grinning.

'Is an IV line illegal in pumpkin circles? Like doping in sport?'

'We cut the stalk away,' Jake said. 'The evidence is rotting in Angus's compost patch. And I doubt they've invented a urine test for pumpkins.'

And then there was another cry of awe and they turned—to see another pumpkin being hauled across the judging area.

A huge pumpkin. Vast!

Bigger than Spike?

'Whose…?' Kirsty breathed, and a head bobbed up from behind the pumpkin and beamed.

Ben Boyce.

'Hi,' he said, and he looked at Angus and his beam darned near split his face.

'You—you…' For a moment Kirsty thought Angus was heading for apoplexy. She moved toward him, but Angus's face was recovering his colour, turning the healthy red of true indignation. 'You traitor!'

'Why traitor?' Ben said—all innocence. 'I grew my pumpkin in my back yard and you grew yours in yours. What's the harm in that?'

'You helped with my pumpkin!'

'So I did,' Ben said. His wife was firmly tucked by his side and he was walking with a step that was almost sprightly, totally at odds with the gnarled appearance of his arthritis-affected bones. 'It wouldn't have been sporting not to have helped.' He beamed again as his pumpkin was hoisted onto the scales. 'Her name's Fatso, by the way,' he told them. 'And she's a better doer than Spike. Thirstier.'

Angus gasped. 'You don't meant to tell me you used IV lines.'

'Of course we did,' Ben said. 'When you started using them I got some medical advice. We watched Doc McMahon do yours and my Maggie's a nurse. We owe you a vote of thanks, Doc,' he told Kirsty, who choked.

Unnoticed—or maybe noticed but unobtrusive—Jake's arm came around her waist.

'Fatso will have to win,' Susie was saying. She lifted Rosie out of her baby sling and perched her small, wrinkled person on top of the pumpkin. Cameras went wild. 'Oh, Angus, do you mind very much?'

Angus was glowering at his friend. 'Of course I mind,' he barked at Ben. 'Whippersnapper. That's eight out of twenty times you'll be beating me. You wait until next year!'

Next year.

Kirsty blinked. This from a man who just weeks ago had intended to die.

'It's a date, then,' Ben said. 'Same time next year, Angus Douglas, and it's a bottle of your best Scotch against one of Maggie's fruit cakes that I'll beat you again.'

'Done.'

General laughter. Angus slapped his friend on the back and they headed to the refreshment rooms—probably for one of Angus's whiskies.

Laughter being the best medicine?

Tomorrow being the best medicine.

'It's time for the mother-daughter sack race,' someone announced over the loudspeaker.

Jake's hand dropped from her waist.

He moved over to where Alice and Penelope were admiring the pumpkins. 'Let's go find a lemonade, girls,' he told them.

All around them women were sorting themselves into groups. Kirsty watched for a few minutes. This seemed to be a general mother-daughter sack race, the only rule being that mothers and daughters had to be in the same sack.

The sacks were piled high, a huge assortment of weird-sized sacks.

The mother-daughter combinations were extraordinary.

There were ancient mothers with almost-as-ancient daughters. One mother had three daughters. One mother had five daughters! Mavis was there, Kirsty saw in astonishment. She'd been wheeled along in a wheelchair. Now someone was frantically cutting holes in a sack for her wheelchair, and Barbara was preparing to climb in with her. There was also Barbara's daughter and two more grandkids Kirsty hadn't seen before.

'Hey, I can do that,' Susie said. She'd come in her wheelchair—only because she still needed a walking stick and she couldn't carry Rosie or stay upright very long without it. 'I'm a mother, and if Mavis can do it, so can I.'

'Yahoo!' someone yelled—it was Mrs Grey from the post

office, wielding a vast pair of scissors. She picked up a sack and prepared to chop wheel holes. 'You and Rosie'll knock 'em dead, girl.'

Susie and Rosie would race.

Mother and daughter.

Kirsty went to help—and then she paused. There were lots of people helping Susie.

She looked across the fairground and saw Jake retreating.

He was leaving. He was taking his girls to the lemonade stall so Penelope and Alice would ask no questions.

Questions like why didn't they have a mother?

He wouldn't push, she thought. He had a twin by each hand, gripping hard, and the slumping of the girls' shoulders said they were aware of what was happening and they hated it.

If she called out…

Could she?

Why not? Why on earth not?

The rest of her life started now.

'Alice,' she yelled. 'Penelope!'

They turned. They all turned.

Alice and Penelope looked hopeful.

'Do you girls want to come in a sack with me?' she yelled— and every person there knew exactly what she was saying. Every person in the fairground knew their local doctor, and almost every one of them wished for exactly this.

Jake was standing motionless. Expressionless. She dared give him no more than a fleeting glance but in that moment she knew she'd crossed some invisible line, and there was no going back.

'You're not our mother,' Alice called, straight to the point like any four-year-old should be.

'No, but a mother-daughter sack race is fun,' Kirsty called back. 'So I thought…I could be a friend who's a sort of mother-when-you-need-me.'

How about that for a declaration? she thought, breathless. Even her twin was hornswoggled. Susie and her chair were halfway into her sack. Susie sat with her mouth open, and the twins stared with their mouths open, and Kirsty thought, There are far too many twins.

There's too much emotion.

But not for long. People were starting to cheer. Someone— Ben?—hauled an extended-family sack from the pile, and the twins dropped their father's hands and ran. They dived into Ben's proffered sack, whooped around the bottom for a bit and then stood, sack pulled to their chins, with a gap left in the middle.

'This is your place,' Penelope told Kirsty. 'In the middle.'

'That's where all the best mothers go,' Susie said softly from beside her. 'Jump right in, Kirsty, love. Heart and all.'

So she did. The next minute she was in the sack with the twins, lined up in a row stretching right across the fairground.

The assortment was stunning. There were womenfolk from Rosie's age to Mavis's age, and everything in between. Mothers of all shapes and sizes.

Alice and Penelope were beaming and beaming, but not Kirsty. Kirsty stared straight ahead while Jake stared at the ground. Kirsty caught a glimpse of Angus patting him on the shoulder, and all of a sudden she felt like crying.

There'd been enough tears.

'Go!'

They were off. Jumping, running, wheeling, tumbling, mothers and assorted daughters, up to four generations in the one sack, all making their way any way they knew how to get to the finish line.

The menfolk were roaring encouragement and advice. Angus had forgotten all about his lack of oxygen, his dicky heart, and he was cheering fit to burst.

Kirsty and Penelope and Alice were concentrating. 'We have to jump in step,' Kirsty gasped at their third tumble. There were some fast movers here but the fastest were being handicapped in all sorts of ways: dogs racing across their paths—including Boris!—people falling over; an ex-marathon runner and her sprinter daughter being held back by the local black-smith who simply darted over and stood on a corner of their sack until his wife and kids passed them by.

'We're jumping, we're jumping,' the twins were yelling. 'Watch us jump, Daddy.'

'Go on,' Kirsty heard herself scream. 'We can do this.'

She could do this.

Of course she could. And of course they did. They reached the finish maybe eighteenth, maybe nineteenth, but glori-ously in the middle of the pack and not at the back. They watched in a muddle of sacks and contorted bodies and frantic laughter as someone rushed forward and proclaimed Susie and Rose—*Susie and Rose!*—as the winners. In their chair they'd been out front by a mile, and second were Mavis and Barbara and assorted granddaughters. Someone was laughing and saying that next year the wheelchairs had to be nobbled, but not this year. This year the wheelchairs were the winners.

There were more winners than wheelchairs.

Kirsty lay on the ground and hugged her girls to her and Boris bounded over and licked her face, and she wondered how she could feel any more of a winner than she did right now.

Then Jake was there.

He was crouching down, lifting her out of the puddle of children and sack and dog—*doctor performs incision of sack with precision and style*—hauling her against him and laughing and kissing her and smiling his pride and his joy for all to see.

'We didn't win, Daddy,' Alice was saying.

'We didn't win,' echoed her twin. 'But we jumped really high.'

'Don't you worry about winning,' Jake told his daughter in a voice that was none too steady. 'There's always next year.'

And then in front of the entire population of Dolphin Bay, in front of these people who would be part of their lives for ever, Dr Jake Cameron kissed Dr Kirsty McMahon.

Two became one.

Or…two became part of this wonderful, muddly assorted population that was what you called life.

For ever.

0606/03a

MILLS & BOON®

Live the emotion

_MedicaL
romance™

THE MIDWIFE'S SPECIAL DELIVERY
by Carol Marinelli

It has been three years, but gorgeous doctor
Rory Donovan is back. Midwife Ally Jameson is
determined that she won't lose her heart to him a
second time, yet surrounded by the joy of the baby
ward, it is hard for Ally not to remember the love
they once shared. Especially when Rory is so caring
and gentle with her.

A BABY OF HIS OWN *by Jennifer Taylor*

Bachelor Dads – Single Doctors…Single Fathers!

Connor Mackenzie was the love of nurse Lucy
Adams's life. But when it came to a choice between
her or his career, Connor chose the job – and left
her pregnant! Lucy doesn't know the real reason he
left. She doesn't know how much he has missed her.
And she doesn't know how determined he is to be a
father to their child!

A NURSE WORTH WAITING FOR
by Gill Sanderson

Six years ago, apprentice nurse Jan Fielding was in
love with Chris Garrett, newly qualified doctor.
Until Chris was caught up in a mountain accident
involving her father, and the results changed her
life forever. Now, working together on a Mountain
Rescue team, the feelings that Jan thought were
gone begin to surface once more.

On sale 7th July 2006

*Available at WHSmith, Tesco, ASDA, Borders, Eason,
Sainsbury's and most bookshops*

www.millsandboon.co.uk

MILLS & BOON®

0606/03b

Live the emotion

Medical
romance™

THE LONDON DOCTOR *by Joanna Neil*

Dr Hannah accepted a position in a busy London
A & E department for one reason only – to track
down her real mother. But working with handsome
Dr Adam Driscoll was proof that city life could be
very exciting! Could this doctor be the one to help
Hannah finally face a future filled with love?

EMERGENCY IN ALASKA *by Dianne Drake*

Dr Aleksandra Sokolov loves working in Alaska
– a harsh but beautiful environment that tests her
skills to the limit. The new doctor in her territory,
Michael Morse, may be charming his patients, but
not Alek. Alek won't confront her feelings for
Michael. But when an avalanche threatens their lives,
their passion is unleashed…

PREGNANT ON ARRIVAL *by Fiona Lowe*

Air Rescue:
High flying doctors – High altitude medical drama

Dr Bronte Hawkins is a new recruit on the
Muttawindi Flying Doctors team. Huon Morrison
is a Flight Doctor scarred by the mistakes of others.
He is confident that with Bronte on his team
they will be the best – as long as he can keep his
feelings for her under control! Until a routine check
unsettles both Huon and Bronte's dreams – Bronte
is pregnant…

On sale 7th July 2006

Available at WHSmith, Tesco, ASDA, Borders, Eason,
Sainsbury's and most bookshops

www.millsandboon.co.uk

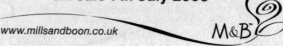

FREE!
4 Books
and a surprise gift!

We would like to take this opportunity to thank you for reading this Mills & Boon® book by offering you the chance to take FOUR more specially selected titles from the Medical Romance™ series absolutely FREE! We're also making this offer to introduce you to the benefits of the Reader Service™—

- ★ FREE home delivery
- ★ FREE gifts and competitions
- ★ FREE monthly Newsletter
- ★ Exclusive Reader Service offers
- ★ Books available before they're in the shops

Accepting these FREE books and gift places you under no obligation to buy, you may cancel at any time, even after receiving your free shipment. Simply complete your details below and return the entire page to the address below. You don't even need a stamp!

putting the One minute manager to work